ONE MISTAKE

FRAT HOUSE SCANDAL
BOOK THREE

SUMMER COOPER

LOVY BOOKS

PROLOGUE

Reese

I kidnapped Ryder Kennedy.

Kidnapped.

Ryder.

Kennedy.

On a whim. Because I was drunk. And he'd walked out of the bar's backdoor, right next to my car. Opportunity. And stupidity. Drunkenness. The availability of a taser. History. All of these factors added up to one stupid move. But a move I'd dreamed of since…a decade ago.

It was chance really. Not my fault. I'd been back in Glouster less than a week. Cleaning out my mom's apartment. Hadn't had a drink in ten years. Not a single sip of anything alcoholic. But then I'd seen him. Walking into the backdoor of a bar. Oblivious. Head high. Like he ruled the world. And tequila came calling.

Had I gone blind, I would've known those striking

features—eyes so blue the oceans had to be weeping with jealousy, long legs, Brad Pitt hair. And it wasn't really his fault he hadn't recognized me. I'd traded my mousy blonde hair for locks I refused to cut but braided and colored this week to Marilyn Monroe platinum. I'd exchanged all my calf-length skirts and sensible shoes for heels and miniskirts that didn't leave much to the imagination. And I'd gone from fresh-faced to full model makeup with tattooed arms and black fishnet stockings. No one did undercover hooker better than me.

But in one split-second bad decision, I threw all my years of hard work, all my training, straight down the toilet, gave it a good a righteous flush then swayed drunkenly as it circled the drain.

Thank God, I wasn't too drunk to recognize I needed help. I called in the troops then stood beside the car until they arrived. Together. Good thing because I needed one of them to take my keys and drive my precious cargo to... somewhere...since I could safely say, I wasn't making the best decisions right then.

Felicity Fields-Makenzie and Avery Shaw stepped from opposite sides of Felicity's Prius then came around to stand in front of me. "He's in the trunk?" She tapped a few times on the hatch while I nodded. "Why? What the fuck were you thinking, Reese?"

"I don't know. I just...did it." A tequila-fueled, spur-of-the-moment kidnapping. A prosecutor would have a field day with that one.

"So, undo it. Open the damned thing. Let him out. We'll set him on the sidewalk and you can go home and pretend you've never been here." Felicity shook her head and caught her long brown hair in her hand, laid it neatly over her shoulder then stroked it. Nervous habit. It had always annoyed me when I was sober, but drunk I thought it looked kind of elegant. Drunk me was obviously not so bitter about life. "You can't keep him. You have to let him go."

Probably a valid suggestion. One I should've agreed to so as not to make a bad situation worse. And for her information, it wasn't about keeping him. Although…"Counter offer. We take him back to Mom's place"—calling it my place just didn't feel right—"and we could…" That was where the plan went awry.

* * *

Ryder

I WAS IN A TRUNK. I knew it was a trunk by the close confines, and the fact it smelled like gasoline, and I had a tire iron jammed into my back. What I didn't know was how and or why I'd gotten there. Last thing I remembered, I'd locked up the bar, carried the trash to the dumpster, and…nope. That was it.

There wasn't much room to move in this thing, but I tried. Valiantly tried. Cramped for the effort.

And when I settled down and the pain subsided, I could hear voices.

He's not a puppy you can just keep, Reese. Reese? Couldn't be. Not after all these years. But one fuck of a coincidence to be in a trunk possibly belonging to another woman named Reese who might or might not have had a reason to stuff me into said trunk.

Who said anything about keeping him? Uh-oh. That didn't sound good.

Then what? What's your plan? Kill him?

Objection.

I can't be part of a killing. I have a nervous stomach. A new fresh voice. Scared. I could use that. Maybe.

Dump him in the ocean?

What the fuck? Whoever that one was, she had an evil streak.

No. I think it's time Captain Video learned his lesson.

"Captain Video." For hell's sake. It'd been ten years. I'd lost my inheritance. My car. My family. I worked in a bar where I served drinks to rich assholes who treated me like the help. Lesson learned already.

Reese

Avery drove like an old woman. Or a teenager just learning to control a car. Hands at ten and two. Seatbelt snug over her shoulder. Blinker on half a block before a turn. Exact speed limit. Dear God. She was a walking advertisement for safety. "You could speed this up."

"Yeah because when we get pulled over, we'll just explain our hurry with 'Sorry, officer, we had to get the guy in the trunk home.'" She shook her head. "I don't know how I let you talk me into this."

I chuckled. "Friendship." One that had lasted through years of separation. Of course, going through something like the Glouster Video Scandal together bonded us. "Plus, I'm adorable." She laughed, so I continued. "And you missed me."

"That I did. Of course, I had no idea you'd gone batshit crazy enough to kidnap Ryder." I almost fell out of the car when she glanced away from the road to me. But the door wasn't open. "What are you going to do with him?"

"I don't know yet." But I was going to think of something.

* * *

Ryder

THE CAR ROLLED to a stop and the motor shut down. Thank God, too, because the exhaust fumes made my stomach toss and roll. And I was about ten seconds from spewing my Philly cheesesteak all over my t-shirt.

The voices were back. *Do you have your taser?*

There was a laugh. A tinkle of a drunken giggle. Familiar. Tequila shooter girl? *I have this.*

Holy shit, Reese. That's a gun.

Of course, it's a gun. I'm a cop. It came with the uniform.

Reese the cop. Not when I got through with her.

You're insane and we're all going to prison. I'm too pretty for prison. They'll pass me around like candy.

Real panic. Good. But not a voice I recognized.

No one's going to prison. Probably.

Oh, fuck.

Just help me get him out of here. Then you guys can go. No one has to know you're involved.

Wrong. So, so wrong.

* * *

Reese

AVERY REACHED to open the trunk and Felicity stopped her with a hand on her shoulder. "Wait." She looked around Mom's backyard and finally reached to pick up a hand spade Mom had probably used to plant the neat rows of flowers Avery'd driven over on her way to the back patio.

"Digging this, huh?" Avery and I looked at Felicity. Someone had to tell her that her puns weren't so funny anymore, but now probably wasn't the time since I needed her help. Plus, I was drunk enough that I laughed at her joke.

"Open it." I aimed my Glock at the back of the car. The safety was on. He wasn't in danger, but he didn't need to know it.

She popped the hatch, and he groaned. A shiver of a memory ran through me and settled in my panties. The sound of heaven. Shit.

"Focus, Reese." Avery shoved me.

"Get out," I whispered the words because I was still caught in a memory so potent I might have been near orgasm on the lawn. I could only see the back of his head, the long line of his neck, and the wide breadth of his shoulders. All familiar. Too familiar. And not something I should have been concentrating on. Definitely shouldn't have been wondering if he tasted the same, if he still moaned low and deep when…shit.

He used his upper body to pull himself up and twist around so he could unfold himself to stand in front of us. "Wait." He was too big, too unpredictable to not restrain. I shoved my hand into my shoulder bag and rooted blind until my fingers scraped against the metal cuffs. I handed them to Avery. "Put these on him. Behind his back."

"No. You're out of your mind." Avery held up both hands and took a step back. "I'm not going to Shawshank for you. I saw that movie. It's a bad place." Her eyes went wide, and she bit her lower lip. Lord, she watched too much TV. It was her escape from grading poorly written term papers. Plus, she had a mad crush on Morgan Freeman.

"That's a fictional prison created by Stephen King for *fictional* purposes." I rolled my eyes and rattled the cuffs at her again. "Come on. I can't hold the gun and cuff him."

"There's really a Shawshank Prison in Ohio." Felicity, our little trivia buff. But she shoved the hand spade under her arm and snatched the cuffs out of my hand. "God, Avery. We're already in this deep. You drove the getaway car."

"Don't listen to your little friend. If you let me go now, you haven't done anything wrong. Not that I'll report anyway." Sharper, meaningful, he added, "Avery Shaw. Felicity Makenzie. Reese Winthrop."

And I might've been drunk, but I was sober enough to know this was bad.

* * *

Ryder

REESE WINTHROP.

Wow.

Not the Reese Winthrop I knew ten years ago. Well, maybe like the one I'd met in the bar back then, but not the one I'd gotten to know. Not the one…

1

Reese

$\mathscr{I}$ was ten years younger the last time I saw him.
I'd been naïve and stupid, then broken. By him.
By Ryder Kennedy. And back then he'd been larger than
life. Not just in size. Although he came in at a respectable
six-four. Large in personality. Large in social status. Large
in life.

Today, he looked small. Beaten by the life that once
upon a time, he'd had by the balls. And it made my heart
glad. Because along with being larger than life, Ryder
Kennedy had been an asshole, a womanizer, a liar, and in
my humble opinion, one not shared by the great state of
Maine, a criminal.

And by *beaten by life* I didn't mean his clothes—a pair of
jeans that hugged his thighs and still remarkably tight ass,
or the long-sleeved gray Henley that hid the Alpha Alpha
Phi tattoo on the inside of his left forearm and managed to

make his eyes look bluer than I knew they already were. *Beaten by life* referred to the new and lovely, well-deserved haunted look in his eyes. The slouch of his shoulders. The overall downtrodden attitude. All of it delighted me, too.

I stared at him. This was such a bad idea. Why I didn't drink anymore. Drinking made me do stupid shit. Namely Ryder Kennedy. Which was why I'd gotten the hell out of Glouster. Away from the college, the fraternity, the scandal that rocked our alma mater to its foundation and almost landed Ryder, Finn, Keaton, and Jameson—the Glouster Four—in jail.

He stared back at me. "How long have you been planning this?"

I chuckled. "About a minute before I tased you."

"Bullshit."

"Does this look well-planned to you?" He was handcuffed to the bed, his feet tied to the footboard with a pair of mom's old nylons. Nothing about this spoke to a criminal mastermind. I breathed out a long, slow, and much-needed huff then waited as if being a few feet from the man who took my virginity was nothing to be anxious over.

He jerked against the cuffs, then when the metal spindle he was attached to didn't bend or break, he settled down. "Why are you doing this?" He spoke in a resonant, deep, voice, one I'd heard purr and growl, a voice that, even though I hated its owner, made my pussy wet. Unfortunately, I didn't have drunken stupidity to explain that one away. But it could work for the kidnapping since I didn't have any other valid excuse. "Because you overserved me at the bar last night."

He laughed. Humorless. Flat. "You tase me, shove me in a trunk, almost suffocate me in your shitty car with the leaky exhaust, drag me to this shit hole, and it's my fault?"

Oh, it was definitely his fault. I just couldn't quite explain how. Yet.

I didn't take exception to his classification of my mom's house. To someone who grew up on the Kennedy estate in the Hampton Hills section of Glouster, Mom's two-bedroom bungalow on the more affordable side of town probably seemed like quite the step down.

"What can I say? I was drunk." A burst of air rumbled through the overhead vent and shook my head. For the love of all that was holy. Couldn't he at least have had a pointed ear, a giant wart, some slight imperfection I could concentrate on?

"Juries don't give a fuck if you're drunk." He scoffed and shook his head, his gaze locked with mine. "You're going to prison."

I went for the metaphorical jugular. "Oh, that's right. You were prelaw before you decided to go dark side and post videos of your friends getting laid." And because I wanted to remind him of who he was as much as what he did, I smiled. "How's that almost law degree working out for you, bartender?"

"What the hell happened to you?" He broke the gaze and turned away.

"You did." The fucking truth of it.

He glared at me. "I can't believe I got kidnapped by bad girl Barbie."

Bar girl Barbie? "Were you expecting to be kidnapped by a Schwarzenegger or a Stallone?"

"Didn't really expect to get kidnapped." He looked me up and down. "A strong wind could take you."

I was a respectable five-seven without the two-inch heel on my boots. And I worked out. And I knew how to take down a monster twice my size and three times my weight. I was good at my job. Protector of the abused woman—once, with the lucky swing of a baseball bat, I kicked a mean husband ass. And once, in a right place right time situation, I pinned a jewel thief I'd been hunting between my front bumper and a wall while I sat in my car polishing off a chipotle chicken wrap and waited for backup. And there was the time I walked right into a cult compound and dragged out the fourteen-year-old daughter of a desperate mother then fended off the cult leader with his own shovel I found leaning against a tree on my way out. So yeah. I could handle myself.

And I didn't one bit like him questioning it. After all, he was the one tied to the bed. My mind flashed to one of my favorite Ryder Kennedy fantasies, and I stood and sexy-walked toward him.

I leaned in and let my lips hover near his ear. Jesus, he smelled good—citrus and sandalwood—and I lowered my voice so he couldn't hear how badly I wanted him. But not because he was Ryder Kennedy, and I'd spent a lot of nights alone in bed with my vibrator thinking of his hands, his mouth, and his dick. By this point, any man would've done the job. "I like my odds."

But I still didn't have a plan. And if I wanted to keep my job and stay out of jail, I was going to have to come up with one soon.

One Decade Ago

"BUT IT'S YOUR BIRTHDAY!" Every year for the last three, Beth Cooper and I engaged heartily in the exact same argument.

I nodded. Not because I agreed with anything else she said but because it was indeed my birthday. "Yeah. And I'm going to curl up on this sofa with my blanket and my bottle of chocolate milk and watch ten hours of Brad Pitt movies and when he yells 'what's in the box' I'm going to pretend it's my head in there."

"Oh, dear God." She shook her head. "Aside from the fact you didn't pick Meet Joe Black or Legends of the Fall, movies where we actually see Brad getting his groove on, I would not be a good friend if I let you stay home alone, pathetic, and virginal on your birthday with chocolate milk and movie screen Brad Pitt when you could be out getting your own groove on with some if-you-drink-enough-he's-a-look-alike."

Oh, for hell's sake. No matter how much tequila I consumed, no one on this campus looked like Brad—the one man I would gladly sacrifice said virginity to—except

Ryder Kennedy. Gorgeous. Sexy. Beautiful and as much out of my league as good old Brad, Ryder Kennedy.

She puffed out her lower lip. "Come on. Take a break. Let loose. Enjoy this time because soon we're going to have to get real jobs and pay our own way. You want lots of tequila-soaked memories to carry you through all that." On her last try, she won me over. "I'll buy."

Beth Cooper never paid for a thing in her life. She was beautiful and witty, so wealthy it was impossible for us common folks to imagine, personable in ways I couldn't even fake, and it worked for her. She never bought her own drinks, or dinners, or paid a cover anywhere we went. It would have been easy to hate her if I wasn't the one she chose to shine her star over.

"Come on. Please." Plus, her puppy dog eyes were impossible to say no to.

And she was the complete opposite of me. The anti-Reese. She was trendy. Beth without a mini-skirt and perfectly drawn eyebrows was an unheard of phenomenon —or at least one I'd never seen in four years of college roommating.

My skirts, by comparison, all hit below my knee, my collars were chin height, and the only thing I'd ever drawn on my face were whiskers for a fourth-grade production of Cats.

But trendy or stuck in a nineteen-sixties wardrobe disaster, I didn't do bars. Ever. "I just want to stay in."

"Look, Reese. I have to be honest with you." Now she put on her serious face—thin lips, wide eyes, slight nostril flare. "This virginity thing is weighing you down. Pretty girl like you should let her hair down." She pulled the elastic holding my bun in place. "Dance on a table. Find some hot bar guy and do a body shot." She stood and paced. "I mean, you're not getting the college experience your parents are paying for. You need a wild night. You need to take hot body shot guy and let him bang your head into his headboard until you see stars."

Oh good. So in her crazy scenario, I had a concussion to look forward to. "Beth..."

"You dress like a nun and you're never going to get laid." She stopped pacing and swiped her forehead. "There. I said it."

Rude. Other people besides those who dedicated their lives to God wore sensible shoes. "I'm dressing for the job I want." A no-nonsense legal genius. Plus, dressing this way was the only form of rebellion my free-spirited, Daisy-duke short wearing, free-spirited mother recognized.

She clucked her tongue against her teeth. "I know. All you're missing is the rosary and one of those head veil things." And maybe she was right, but this was who I was. I didn't know how to be anything else. Nor did I own any clothes that would make any different kind of statement than *peace be with you, my child.* "Come on. One makeover. One night. One fabulous fucking memory, Reese. I promise you won't regret it."

Since I didn't have much more to lose than a couple hours of sleep, and she never really asked anything of me, I nodded. "Fine, you win."

"Really?" She squealed and hugged me. And it took two hours after that to make me presentable enough even I didn't recognize me. My hair curled around my shoulders, and I had eyebrows and lashes I never noticed before. My lips were lined and my cheeks were blushed, and one wrong breath was going to cause a Janet Jackson wardrobe malfunction, but I felt pretty, and confidence was half the battle. At least, according to Beth.

And I actually liked the club. Music pumped through the speakers and lights bounced off the walls and the ceiling and the hundred or so people gyrating on the dance floor. It only took three drinks for me to feel the vibe. For the music to inspire me. For my feet to tap and my shoulders to sway. Three drinks for the alcohol to take hold and make me not care that I had zero rhythm and even less grace.

I also knew the rule about not peaking too early into the evening, but I didn't care about that either. And that was how I ended up crashing into Ryder Kennedy. And, oh hello, he smelled good—citrus and sandalwood and man. I might've taken an extra deep breath before I moved back.

"Hi." I couldn't hear him over the music, but I could see what he said.

"Hey." I couldn't hear myself either, but hoped I sounded sultry and sexy.

He still had his arms around me, and no way was I taking another step back until I had to. My heart was pounding, and my vision blurred at the edges. I didn't know if it was from his body touching mine or if the alcohol was doing its thing, but in the moment, I didn't give a shit. Someone had his arms around me, and it felt nice. I cared about that.

And that someone was Ryder Kennedy. Looking at me. Touching me. His thumb under the hem of my shirt caressing my spine where the waistband of this skirt hit. No way did I want to ruin that.

Heat rolled down my skin from my cheeks to my toes and everywhere in between while my heart throbbed in time with the music and my body matched tempo. I almost moaned.

"Do I know you?" His breath warmed my ear, and my knees went weak.

Of course, he knew me. We'd been partners in BIO101 freshman year, and I sat in front of him in POLISCI. Plus, we were both prelaw, so we spent Monday through Thursday in a lot of the same classes.

"I don't think so." True enough. He didn't know this me. The one who cared what he thought. The one who wanted him. And maybe it was the alcohol, but I wanted him to want me back. To want the girl in Beth's sequined top and thigh-high black boots with the bows on top where they almost met the tiny little skirt I borrowed. I wanted to look back on my deathbed and know I gave my virginity to Ryder Kennedy.

I let the thought hop into the driver's seat, and I pulled his head down—he was pretty damned tall. Before I spoke, I dragged my tongue along his earlobe to the top and back down. "I want you to fuck me."

He chuckled but his arm tightened around my waist. "Okay." And he lowered his head to kiss me, to press his full, soft lips against mine, to caress my mouth with his until my breath, when it came, huffed out in short loud puffs of air. To say he knew how to kiss was an understatement. And to say he knew how to tease a nipple through a shirt until I gasped again, and my panties melted wasn't an exaggeration either.

He smiled against my mouth and pulled me into the shadowed corner still in the crowd but at the edge. Nothing in my life felt so sexy or so decadent as standing in a room full of people who were all ignoring his fondling me for their own bits of fondling one another. And it was amazing. Erotic in ways I didn't understand.

Right up to the minute he pulled back and slipped his fingers through mine. Then we were off. Across the dance floor. Out the door. To his car in the parking lot. Not a car. An SUV with a big backseat he helped me into then climbed in behind.

It all happened fast. Too fast. He unfastened the neck of my halter top and moved his lips down my throat to my left breast while his hand slid up the inside of my thigh. This wasn't the story I waited twenty-two years for. Not one I wanted to see at the end when my life flashed before my eyes one final time. No way was I surrendering my v-card in the back of an Escalade. Neither did I want to pull the brakes. But there was a way to salvage this. I'd done it before with Robby Winstead in tenth grade. Then a couple of times after when I'd chickened out of sex.

Still bare from the waist up, I pushed his hands away so I could get to the area I needed to get to. I unfastened his belt, then his button-fly, concentrating on the scent of his car. It smelled like money, or more that he spent a lot of money to make it smell good.

I breathed in deep and took him into my mouth. He moaned and clenched his fists beside him, then shifted his hips. "Oh, God." He dropped a hand to my shoulder and stroked my throat with his thumb and his grip tightened. And went tighter. And tighter until I moved him away. "Sorry."

I pumped his dick a couple times with my hand before he groaned and came in my mouth. While he breathed out a few wobbly breaths, I moved to sit on the seat next to him and adjusted my top. "Wow." He tucked his cock back into his jeans and fastened the buttons. "Can I see you again?"

I hadn't even told him my name. "Oh, I don't know." Of course, I was going to say yes. I'd been fantasizing about Ryder Kennedy since we'd been partnered in Bio that first year. But I had to save some dignity since I'd just spent ten minutes sucking him off in the back of a car.

"I could cook for you." Instead of answering, I reached for the door handle but didn't climb out because he spoke again. "Hey. I'll be at the marina tomorrow. Slip #19." He cleared his throat. "I'm not going to beg, but I'm going to cook enough for two, so…" He shrugged and leaned in to kiss me softly. "I hope I'll be sharing it with you."

Wow. An invitation by Ryder Kennedy to the Alpha Alpha Phi yacht. Beth was never going to believe this. "I guess we'll see tomorrow." I never felt cooler before in my life than when I climbed out of that SUV.

2

Ryder

I had to piss. But my memory along with the feel of her pressed against me when she leaned in to whisper, gave me a hard-on. Plus, I was still tied and cuffed to the most Godawful bed in the history of discomfort.

Had to be a way out of this. Something I could say to make her let me go. She'd been in and out all day long. With her friends. Keaton's and Finn's girlfriends. Even though I wasn't in the circle of friendship anymore, Glouster was a small enough town I knew who dated who.

I could hear the hum of electrical tools. Hum rather than growl. The fft fft of a nail gun. The occasional vibration of a compressor. When she walked into the bedroom again, a fine sheen of sweat and white dust coated her skin. "Building my cage?"

She ignored me and went to the attached bathroom for

a glass of water. "Here. Drink this." I sat up and sipped while she held the cup. "I need to move you."

Move me? A chance to get the hell out of here. "Okay." I smiled. Cop or not, I could overpower her. Slip out of here. But before I could formulate a get-out jail-free plan, she went for the button of my jeans. Flicked it open. Lowered the zipper. "What the fuck are you doing?" And why the fuck was my cock acting like it was into it?

"I don't want to have to tase you again or drug you. Naked guy won't run as fast as one wearing his Levis." This was my girl who got away. The girl I could close my eyes and still feel pressed against me even after ten years. She still smelled like cinnamon apples, wholesome, sweet, a lie if ever there was one.

"Maybe you don't remember me. But I've spent my fair share of time naked in public." Before I became king of the Alphas, I'd been a pledge. A pledge who bubble-bathed naked in the fountain at the center of campus wearing only a shower cap and nipple clips. A pledge who streaked across the outfield on opening day of baseball season. A pledge who stood up in the middle of PSYCH101, ripped off my tear-away pants, and danced naked out of the room. Apparently, nudity was the theme of my pledge week. Good times.

"You're not twenty years old anymore."

Whatever that meant. I sighed. "Why are you doing this? Because the civil suit got dropped?" The judge kicked the case. Not me. He'd said the plaintiffs had already been paid restitution from the plea deal I took. Mom and Dad probably had something to do with it—a contribution to some legal fund or a pledge for the new courthouse being built—but even if they did, they would never tell me.

She wrinkled her forehead and sat on the bed beside me, letting her hand rest on my thigh. On. My. Thigh.

"I wasn't part of the civil suit." She didn't have a right to be, anyway. The video of us together never made it online.

I shrugged as much as a guy with his arms cuffed over his head could shrug. "I thought maybe you were crusading on their behalf."

"I'm not that noble." She shook her head and another wave of cinnamon apple pie washed over me. My stomach growled. She lifted her hand and curled her finger as it hovered over my stomach before she pulled it back. "Once I move you, I'll get you something to eat."

Was I supposed to be grateful? "That's big of you." I shifted to look at her. Holy shit. Before, I would've never even glanced at a chick with that much ink, but now, close enough I could see the icy blue in her darker blue irises, the line of freckles that arched over her chin, the length of her heavily mascaraed lashes, my dick twitched. Again. Bad Ass Barbie was hot. As hot as she'd been when she'd been the poster girl for virginity.

"Where's your cell phone?" She patted the pockets of my still unfastened jeans, and it was the most attention that area of my body had received in years, so I didn't stop her. When her hands quit moving on their own, I smiled.

"I don't have one." It had been years since anyone wanted to talk to me. I barely had enough money for food and rent. A phone was a pipe dream.

"Really?" Obviously, we had a trust issue between us, but she went back to patting.

"Think about it, Reese. I live in a college town, work in a bar too far away from the college to make money and I'm Ryder Kennedy. Who the hell wants to talk to me?" God, the truth was pathetic. I was pathetic.

She stood. "That is a sad tale, Ryder. Am I supposed to feel sorry for you?" The bitterness was back. But so were the hands at the waistband of my jeans, tugging. And she leaned over, her long hair brushing across my crotch, over my zipper as she struggled, and I pushed my ass harder into the mattress. She pushed her hands under my ass, and I used my weight to hold her there, her hands inside my jeans, against my bare ass.

And somehow, the karma that had been punishing me for the last ten years shifted. "Fuck." When she finally gave up, she tried to stand, but somehow, the zipper of my pants caught her hair and wasn't letting go. She wrapped her hand around the hair stuck in my pants and pulled. But it was really stuck in there. Plus, all the jerking and tugging, the jeans rubbing, made the tip of my dick wet. Made me remember. And oh what a memory it was.

One Decade Ago

I CHECKED my phone for the tenth time in ten minutes. She wasn't coming. And I told myself I didn't care. Instead, I went back to work, leveling the camera aimed at the bed, and using my laptop to make a couple more adjustments to the robotic arm. This thing was fantastic, and any other time I would've appreciated the genius behind it. But right now, my dick was in charge of my brain, and I was stuck on a chick who wasn't coming.

No. I had to focus. Me and the boys had a plan. And this was my part. Keaton supplied the boat. Jameson the robotics. Finn was going to be the supper stud. And I was the computer genius.

Keaton's dad left his fifty-foot yacht—the Love Shack—docked here for us. He said we needed a place to bring our dates that didn't smell like old beer and socks. And none of us—not me, Keaton, Finn, or Jameson—were going to argue. No one argued with Richard Shaw.

Plus, this boat had already bumped Keaton's sex life to legendary status. Before the yacht, he was the quarterback and got more than his fair share of cheerleader pussy, but now, he was getting laid so much he was almost never in class, never at the frat house, and he came into practice with a blonde on one arm and a red bull in the other hand.

But the cameras were for pledge week. An epic pledge week.

I checked the clock again. Not even five minutes since the last time. And I felt like a fool. I hadn't even bothered to get her name. Hadn't reciprocated the holy fuck of an orgasm she'd given me. Hadn't made this invitation sound like anything more than an invitation to finish what we'd started. And while I wouldn't mind that, I kind of wanted to get to know her.

I was pathetic enough to be disappointed. I wanted to

see her. Wanted more. Not just having her lips wrapped around my cock—which twitched again thinking of it.

Shit. I refocused on the computer and dialed Keaton's cell.

He answered. "What's up?"

"I need you to go into my room." I walked him through running the set-up program on my computer which would link the cameras to the Alpha house for a live stream. Though he could see and hear me, the sound only went one way. Not a glitch. A way for us to spy on the pledges when we made them bring their dates to the boat.

But when I heard footsteps on the deck above, I hung up without any further instruction to Keaton.

"Hey." Her voice was familiar, but nothing about her full-length skirt, turtleneck in a matching shade of khaki, and shoes my grandma would've loved was familiar.

"Hi." She chuckled, and something about the sound... "Oh, my God. It's you." She'd gone from vixen to virgin. "Holy shit." Last night, she was hot. So fucking hot. The transformation—no, reversion... I couldn't...she was...fuck.

"Yeah. Holy shit. Right?"

Her face closed, shadowed, and I stood. "I'm sorry. I'm just surprised." No way could this be the same girl who rocked my world last night. "Do we have a class together?" Maybe I could remember her name without having to ask. Or maybe I could figure out how to ask without looking like an asshole.

"Yeah. A lot of them. We're both prelaw."

I was a dick. And normally that didn't bother me, but

the sparkle in her eyes that was so bright and so sexy last night at the club I'd seen it from across the dance floor was gone now. My fault, undoubtedly.

"You want a drink or something?" And by something I meant another taste of my cock. Apparently, it didn't care what she looked like. Plus, I wanted to know if the clothes and the confidence versus her shy girl behavior made a difference in how she…performed.

"A drink would be good." She looked down at her hands.

I hadn't started our dinner yet because I wasn't sure she was going to come and I could order pizza for just me, but there was always plenty to drink on the boat. I cleared my throat and tried to adjust my hard-on in such a way that I could conceal the action and not scare her away. But all my mind would let me think of was her, her luscious lips, her tongue, those nipples. Fuck. The only adjustment I made was to get harder.

Instead of speaking, I nodded and turned away to head to the galley below deck. She followed then walked through behind me to the bedroom.

"Oh, wow."

Yeah. That was why this place worked. Chicks loved the opulence. The marble, the carved wood, the lights in the ceiling, the big, soft bed with its plush blankets and ten zillion thread count sheets.

I needed a minute to get my shit together, so I took my time checking the fridge. "We have soda, juice, beer, vodka, whisky…"

"I'll take a whisky, neat."

Woah. She dressed like a nun and drank like a sailor. Fucking hot.

I poured our drinks and carried them to the bedroom. And my tongue rolled into a ball.

Naked.

On the bed.

And now, there was no doubt in my mind. This was the girl from last night.

"Well, hello."

She grinned. "Is this okay?"

I sounded like a teenager whose voice hadn't quite managed the big change. "Yeah." *Okay* wasn't even close. Magnificent. A fucking religious experience.

The amount of clothes she'd walked in with, covering the goods, hadn't distracted my memory, but my memory hadn't done her justice. She was luscious. Curved in all the best places. And how the hell had I never noticed how exquisite she was? How her smile lit up her face and made me want to kiss her. Or maybe it had nothing to do with her smile. Maybe I just wanted to kiss her, and any reason would do.

I moved from the doorway to the bed. Three of the longest steps of my life. But finally. So close I could smell her perfume. Apples. Cinnamon. Light. Fresh.

Gloss on her lips. Twinkle in her eye. Tremor of her hand as she took her drink. It all worked against my control. I was every horny guy who'd ever been mesmerized by the pretty girl with the nice rack. My dick was hard enough to cut glass.

She set her tumbler on the bedside table then took mine to sit beside it.

Because the woman I'd been with last night was very different from the one here tonight, I wasn't sure what to expect. Probably something vanilla. Probably missionary. Not that I was going to complain. Or that I wouldn't take a few minutes later on to try to talk some adventure into her. But right now, whatever she wanted was what I planned to give her.

She knee-walked across the bed and dipped her finger into my collar to pull me close, tugging until I climbed onto the bed in front of her.

She chewed her lip, shy now and adorable. "I'm nervous."

Naked and nervous. "That's okay. We have time to work that out."

But she picked up my hand, closed her eyes, and put my palm flat over her heart. "I want you."

Fuck. Satin skin under my palm. A short breath burst from my lungs. Nothing in my life prepared me for the feel of her fingers caressing the back of my head as she stared into my eyes, for the slow rush of adrenaline when she leaned in and I got another whiff of her perfume, for the intensity and speed of my hard-on and the sudden desperation attached to it.

I wanted her in a way I didn't understand. And I didn't have time to figure it out, because if this opportunity passed before I could feel her pussy wrapped around my cock, I wouldn't have a reason left to live. Poetic maybe. Dramatic probably. But real. Intense. So fucking ridiculous

I wanted to snap my own neck, but not until I kissed every inch of her.

I leaned in and crushed our lips together while I dragged my hand from her hip to her rib cage and up. Her nipple pebbled between my fingers, and still, our tongues moved against each other, and her touch trailed over my skin, lifting the hem of my shirt.

We broke apart long enough to yank it over my head, could've been me or maybe it was her, but it didn't matter. We were skin to skin, chest to chest.

I lost my usual finesse, the ability to roadmap my way down her body for the most possible pleasure impact. Instead, instinct took over. Need drove. Primal. Disorienting. Fucking perfect.

I kissed her throat then her jaw then her throat again. Hands in her hair then on her breast then lower and back again. Frenzied. Needy. Desperate to touch all of her.

My hand slipped down her belly then dipped between her legs and...fuck. She was so tight, so wet. And she whimpered when I touched her clit, then she curled her fingers around my wrist and held it there.

But I had to taste her.

And it was like she'd never been licked before. Her body writhed and she cried out with each flick of my tongue. She clenched a handful of my hair, and her thighs pressed against my ears. I didn't care. Not so long as she didn't try to push me away.

Her breaths came shorter, her muscles went tighter, and the way she came—powerful, loud—made me want to bury my cock deep inside of her. I wanted my dick to have the same satisfaction my fingers were getting.

"Holy shit." She chuckled and lifted her arms languidly over her head. "If there's a hall of fame for eating pussy, you're getting a statue." The bawdy talk made my dick even harder.

And I was busy rooting through the bedside table for a condom. Sweet Lord. There weren't any left. Just an empty box. And I had a no glove, no love rule. Fuck!

I slammed the drawer shut. How the hell was there no condoms on a boat named Love Shack?

Finn. That rat bastard. Probably used them all and didn't have the cash to replace them.

As I sat trying to figure out a way to make this work—because what were the chances I'd get a second bite of this apple—the bed shifted, and she nestled her chest against my back as she dangled a five-pack of condoms over my shoulder.

I glanced back. "Aren't you just Miss Prepared?" And thank God for it.

"I wasn't leaving anything to chance."

We didn't spend any more time talking until morning.

3

Reese

*A*very had impeccable timing. And a bag of burgers. What she didn't have was the good sense not to poke the bear. And at this moment, I was the damned bear. Unamused and attached to Ryder's crotch by my hair. I tried to ignore him. To ignore every shift of his hips that brought his dick closer to my face, but there was no way he was doing it on accident, or from discomfort.

She set the bag on the table next to the bed, the same table that had a picture of me and my mother together, and gave my hair a solid jerk. "Ow!"

"I'll get some scissors." Which served me right but made my throat thick. I didn't want a haircut. Especially a chunk from the front. She turned to go for the bathroom and I glanced at Ryder. What kind of god made such a beautiful specimen of a man and let him turn into an asshole like this one? It was a question I'd asked myself a thousand times. I'd asked everyone I knew. Sought out preachers and ministers, even a rabbi, and no one had a sufficient answer.

"As I remember it…" He cleared his throat and twisted his hips again. "You used to like…"

"Shut up." Nope. We were absolutely not walking down that memory lane.

"I was just going to say you used to like a little hair pulling." He pulled his bottom lip between his teeth and sucked in a breath that sounded like a groan. It was his signature move. Sexy. Suggestive. Hot. "I liked it, too." Then the bastard closed his eyes and licked his lips.

I should've looked away. Shouldn't have looked down at his dick. Shouldn't have closed my eyes, remembering the feel of him in my mouth, the taste of him on my tongue. Certainly, shouldn't have moaned.

"You know what else I liked?" His voice was low and deep, soft and smooth.

Thank God, Avery returned before I could answer the question. I didn't even care when she hacked the strands of my hair off because the last thing I needed was to make a fool of myself over him. Again.

"I'm not going to ask." I appreciated that about her, and I nodded as she frowned. "But a good friend would tell." She crossed her arms. "Just saying."

"She wants me." He wiggled his eyebrows and I wanted to punch him. Not because it wasn't true—I definitely still wanted him—but because I'd kicked my bad boy habit a long time ago and he was testing my resolve in ways I didn't think I was strong enough to resist.

"Shut up, Ryder."

"It's okay, sweetheart. I've used the highlight reel of our time together as a kickstarter a few times, myself." He grinned. "No shame."

"If there's really a highlight reel, I swear to God, I'm going to use these very dull scissors and a butter knife to change your religion." God only knew how many videos he had of us. Although, I supposed I should thank him for not putting them on the internet when he loaded all the others of his friends having sex. But a little part of me—a part I buried underneath twenty three tattoos, monthly visits to the salon, and enough eyeliner I could make the eyes of everyone in this room pop—wondered why he hadn't been proud enough to put our…liasons…online.

Before I could come up with something snide, he chuckled. "Only in my memory, babe."

I rolled my eyes, stood, and walked to the door.

"Hey, this is your little criminal enterprise. Where are you going?" Avery's panic would've been comical had she not been right.

I turned never taking my hand off the knob. "To buy a shock collar." Although I couldn't decide who needed it more. Him for all his dirty talk or me for wanting to hear more.

I didn't leave. I couldn't. Not only was her car parked behind mine, but I couldn't make my feet move. My brain and my body wouldn't work together. My brain was screaming at me to give this up, but my body wanted to march back into that room and let him go. I'd watched enough Orange Is The New Black to know I wouldn't do well in prison. Instead, I sat in the chair by the back door.

Felicity came up from the basement, goggles still over her eyes, circular saw in her hand. "Where are the new blades?"

I took an exaggerated look around the kitchen. "At the hardware store."

She shook her head and puffed out her lower lip. "Why aren't you taking this seriously? This was your...thing."

My thing was vibrating with need. "I know."

She'd designed the contraption that would keep Ryder prisoner until I could figure out what to do about him. In the sober light of day, I couldn't believe I'd done this. Could less believe my sober and normally very well put-together friends had gone along with it. Usually, they tempered my craziness. But they'd both been victims of the video scandal, so maybe they wanted a little revenge too. I certainly couldn't judge.

"How long until this thing's ready?"

She chuckled. "It's finished. I was just building a shelf over your dryer." Before I could stop her, or even tell her how unsettling and unsanitary I found it, she hopped onto the counter. "So, did you look at his junk? Did it get better with age?"

"What? It's not wine, Fliss. Penises do not get better with age."

She cocked her head and poured herself a glass of wine. "Of course, they do. Finn's did." She shrugged and smug-smiled me over the rim of her glass. "Or maybe he just uses it better now, but..."

If I had to hear about her sex life one more time, I was

probably going to shrivel into an unused ball of horny nerve-endings. "That's great, Fliss."

"He came home early yesterday." Her eyes rolled back into her head. "I'm not one to brag, but—"

"Yes, you are."

"That's because I have something to brag about. And you could, too. Finn has a friend." A few weeks ago, Keaton had a friend, too. I wasn't about to be some cause of theirs, the single friend who needed a man. No matter how hard they tried.

I shook my head. "I'd rather go in and bang Ryder."

She finished her glass of wine then narrowed her eyes at me. "I knew you saw his junk."

"I might have glanced a bulge, but definitely no skin, fore or otherwise." Despite her crazy insinuation, something about my friends risking prison time to help me brought a tear. "Thank you so much for this, you guys. I know I haven't been around much lately." I lived in a whole other state and was only home now because my mom passed away and I had to deal with this house. "But knowing I can call you guys when I need you..." I sniffed, barely holding it together.

Avery plopped a sandwich in front of me then hugged me from behind. "We'd do anything for you. But if we go to jail, you're my bitch." She kissed my cheek.

They argued for a minute about whose tasty treat I would be before I sighed. Time to make the big move.

One Decade Ago

THE ALPHA HOUSE was like any other frat house on campus. Big. Not at all well kept despite the cleaning service and the gardeners employed by the university. Full of rowdy guys too old to be teenagers, too immature to be men. Except the Alpha house had one thing none of the others did. Ryder Kennedy. The guy I woke up every morning thinking of. The one I went to sleep every night dreaming about. The same guy who ignored my ten or twenty phone calls a day. To say I was desperate was an understatement.

That was because he'd ignored me for three weeks. Three. Fucking. Weeks. Made me pathetic enough to hide behind a two-hundred-year-old oak tree, trying for a glimpse of him.

And there he was. Going deep to catch a ball. Going deep. I had somewhere deep he could go.

And that was the problem. The thoughts. Taking every sentence spoken and unspoken and turning it sexual because I was horny. And it was Ryder's fault. He'd created a monster. And left her to her own devices so her brain could go mushy with innuendo and sex dreams that made her moan out loud. In class. Where he never even glanced my way.

I should have been screaming mad. Heaping abuse on him for taking my virginity and then pulling a Houdini, but I just wanted to see him. I just wanted to feel the way he made me feel that night on the boat.

Pathetic was an understatement. Horny was an under-statement. I, apparently, was an understatement.

One who'd forgotten to keep her eye on the ball and barely ducked out of the way—I picked the wrong moment to forget to hide—as the football sailed close enough I felt the wind of it on my face.

Shit. There was no graceful way to explain hiding behind a tree. None that came to me, anyway.

"Well, hello."

Jameson King was a linebacker. Probably why he'd missed the ball. "Hi."

"Reese, right?"

Holy crap. There must have been some sort of good looks qualification in the Alpha selection process. This one was almost as gorgeous as Ryder, and that he knew my name sent a little tingle along my skin.

"Yeah."

He looked me up and down. "Did you wanna play?"

I wasn't sure we were talking football, and my heart fluttered. "Uh, no. I was just…"

He hugged the ball in front of him and leaned in like he was very interested in what I had to say. "Hiding behind a tree to stare at Ryder?" He looked over his shoulder. "It's for you, dude." He called over his shoulder. "Another one of your groupies."

Fuck. The shame. Utter humiliation. Mortification. My skin burned with it all. Knowing that I wasn't the only one stalking Ryder—no matter what I called it—did nothing to lessen the indignity of this moment. "I was just walking by."

Jameson laughed. Threw his head back. And laughed. "Okay."

Whatever he saw on my face—probably something that

said I was about twelve seconds from throwing up on him —had him backing up a half step.

Before I could react, Ryder started across the yard. I didn't want to watch him. Honestly, I'd humiliated myself enough for one day. For one lifetime. Gawking at him with an open mouth and wet panties wasn't going to do anything to help that. But my tongue swiped over my gaping mouth, making the full circle, and I didn't realize it was out or that my lips were hanging open until Jameson laughed.

Since there was no graceful way to step back into hiding behind my tree—not that it was much good for hiding behind anyway—I smoothed my ankle-length denim skirt, resisted the urge to have a sniff to make sure this wasn't a deodorant fail moment, and cleared my throat like I was going to be able to talk.

All my confidence from the other night, both nights actually, disappeared. No longer was I the girl who'd made him moan my name, the girl who'd kissed every inch of him and had every inch of her own skin kissed by him. If nothing else told me that girl was gone, my shaking hands, dry mouth, and churning stomach screamed it.

He smiled, but it was more of the constipated and trying not to show it variety than the happy to see me kind. "Hey."

"Hey." I could be cool. Despite the sweat rolling down my back. Despite my shaking hands.

"I was gonna call you."

No, he wasn't. Or he would have. But I nodded, letting him have his lie. I stood there like a bobblehead doll, nodding and grinning like a fool. I couldn't explain the grin. Not in a way that didn't make me look more pathetic and ridiculous than I already did.

I motioned to the sidewalk. "I was just walking by and saw you guys playing. I wasn't like…" Oh, what was the word? "… stalking you or anything." *Liar, liar. Pants on fire.*

He chuckled. "I didn't think you were."

Well, not in the most technical sense of the word anyway.

We stood glancing at everything but each other, eyes never resting long in one spot until I fidgeted into him. His arms shot out to steady me, presumably so I didn't take him to the ground and land on top of him. But his hand lingered on my hip before he let me go.

"I should go."

He nodded and stepped back. "Okay." But I didn't move and neither did he. "Do you want to get a coffee?"

I wanted to spend every minute of every day looking at him, and if I had to drink sludge, then I'd put some sweetener in it and mix it with some creamer before I slurped the steaming brew. "Sure."

We walked away from the frat house toward town. He kept his hands shoved in his pocket even though I left mine dangling at my side, just in case he wanted to lace our fingers together. Which, clearly, he did not.

After a few blocks of silence, he looked over at me. "I have to ask you something, and it's kind of embarrassing."

He'd seen me naked, licked some pretty private spots, and heard me beg for more. The embarrassment ship already left the harbor. "Okay."

Instead of speaking, he nodded and blew out a breath, but kept walking. Whatever it was, this embarrassing question, seemed relatively serious. "I know we had sex, and I probably should've asked you before then, but…" He scoffed. "But I'm an idiot."

Oh… "I've never…before you, I mean, had sex, so you don't have anything to worry about…medically." Oh, Lord. That *was* on the embarrassing side of things.

He chuckled. "I knew that, but… when you go to the doctor and you fill out the forms that ask for your history, what's the name you put at the top of the page?"

My name. I laughed, relieved. A question I couldn't mess up or make sound lame. "Reese. Reese Winthrop." To be honest, I'd so much liked when he'd called me baby it never occurred to me that he hadn't called me anything else and hadn't asked if he should.

He stopped on the sidewalk and held out his hand, formal and smiling. "Reese. I like it. And it's very nice to meet you."

I slid my palm against his.

Two hours later, we were back at the boat, naked, sweating, ready for round three or maybe it was four. But every kiss, every time he whispered my name, made me want more and he didn't seem inclined to stop either, so when we fell asleep later, all was right with the world.

4

Ryder

What started as a joke...because being kidnapped by a woman I slept with ten years ago had to be a joke, ended up with me being tethered to a wall in a basement of a house that was still better than my shitty apartment. It came with a refrigerator stocked with soda, beer, lunchmeat, and snack cakes. Also, I could walk to the bathroom without needing Reese, almost make it to the steps, and to the washer/dryer combo. I had cable TV—hence the better than my apartment—a pillow top mattress and a stereo that responded to voice commands.

By my third day in captivity, I'd made a plan for escape. I had to get back to work before I lost my jobs, otherwise, I might've been more inclined to stay, to enjoy the afternoon card games with Reese, to hear her recaps of what I'd missed over the weeks of TV programming on her favorite reality shows.

The last couple of days, she'd puttered around, checking on me like a hotel concierge, treating me like a guest as much as a prisoner. If she let me go soon, I would be sure to mention her kindness at her kidnapping trial.

The squeal of hinges announced her arrival and I ignored the uptick in my heart rate. No way was I looking forward to seeing her. Not unless she was setting me free today. The armful of groceries said she wasn't.

She didn't speak as she walked past me. Not even as she pulled a six-pack of beer from the bag and opened one for a long…long drink. I didn't want to care. "You okay?"

Her sigh coupled with an eye roll was answer enough. "I'm a cop."

"You're a felon."

"Careful when that glass house tumbles, big boy." She cocked an eyebrow and gave me a once-over. My skin burned everywhere her gaze touched. This was the look of a woman with wants and needs. And that was information I could use.

"Sorry. You were saying?" I smiled and cocked my head so the dim light here caught my eyes, hopefully giving the illusion of sparkle.

"Never mind." She took another long drink then cracked open a bag of pretzels.

It was hard to be sexy in my T-shirt and basketball shorts that Finn's woman had brought under the rock climber's harness that fit snug over my shoulders and between my legs, but I stood and walked toward her, moved a little too close, let my arm brush against hers, linger a second too long as I took a beer and opened it. The temperature in the room inched up, and I swiped my finger along her lower lip to catch a drop of beer from her last drink. Her eyes flipped open to stare at me. And I stared back because…because I couldn't look away. I was captured and my thumb still tingled.

"I've been waiting all day to talk to someone. To you." Fuck. Her lips pursed and she shook her head. I might've taken that one a little too far.

"Are you flirting with me so I'll let you go home?" She moved away to a spot out of my range of motion. "I'm trying to figure out what to do. I went to the bar and talked to your boss. Flashed my badge and said you were helping the police, so…he seemed okay with waiting for you to come back."

"Yeah. Thanks." Well, she didn't have to do that. And, as a former law student, she should've known that every move she made shoveled another pile of shit onto her heap. She was in over her head already.

I peeked into the bag and pulled out a box of Tastykake cupcakes. My favorite. My mouth dropped open as I turned to look at her. "I can't believe you remembered."

"Not that big of a deal. You ate a whole box of these every day." She protested a little too much. Although I did remember that her favorite dessert was cheesecake smothered in raspberry sauce, that she loved peanut butter everything, and that she hated runny eggs. The intensity of our…relationship made it seem to have lasted longer than its couple of weeks, but it also elevated her above all the other women I'd dated. Etched every detail of our time together in a special place in my mind. And I hadn't realized it until I ended up in her basement, leashed to her wall.

Her cheeks went red, and she looked down. I'd eat a shoe if this wasn't more than just a good deed, if she wasn't feeling all the warm fuzzies I was.

My gut warmed from more than wanting her. Her kindness had always been admirable. I just didn't expect it while she looked like Barbie: the Prison Version.

I moved closer to her, reached out, and threaded my fingers into her hair at the back of her neck. With nothing more than a soft tug, she ended up close enough I could kiss her cheek. Inhale a big whiff of cinnamon apple. Massage her scalp.

She didn't move away. Instead, she slid her hands over my chest. Then as quickly as she lost herself, her eyes cleared, and she pushed me away. But the damage was done and we both knew it. There was no going back now. She'd touched me. Let me touch her and not as part of our kidnapper/kidnap-ee relationship.

"I ordered some, uh, some pizza for dinner." She bent and almost disappeared into the refrigerator as she put the groceries inside.

There had to be a way to make her more comfortable. Get her talking. A safe subject we could bond over. I hadn't given up on the hope of convincing her to set me free, but maybe I wouldn't press charges. Maybe.

"I don't remember you being friends with Avery and

Felicity when we were in school." Her friends seemed a safe subject.

But her eyes flashed. "Well, they helped me pull it together after the whole Beth Cooper thing."

Oh shit. How I'd forgotten about the Beth Cooper Incident—what I'd taken to calling it in my head—I couldn't remember. I should've told her the truth back then. It would've saved her friendship with Beth and not destroyed everything between us.

And I would've told her now had she not turned, crumpled the paper bag in her hands, and stomped to the steps. "I'll bring the pizza down when it gets here."

One Decade Ago

JAMESON AND FINN flanked the sides of my chair. Pledge week was in full swing and the kid on the screen was doing his best to make the chick he was banging scream his name. But she looked kind of bored. Like she would've rather been getting a mani/pedi down at the spa than having this guy grind his tiny tool into her. He grunted on every thrust and she faked a good couple moans before he gave her the goods and rolled off.

"Solid six." Jameson nodded. "He had good form."

Finn leaned his chair on its back legs against the wall and tossed the football in a vertical spiral, caught it then shrugged. "I'm not feeling a six."

I laughed. "Neither was she."

Jameson groaned. "Aww, man. He's trying again." The

kid on the screen was stroking his dick. Pledges got extra points for a repeat performance.

"She's gonna shoot him down." We hadn't had a pledge go for doubles and succeed yet.

Finn set his chair straight with a thud against the floor then leaned closer. He couldn't see shit without his contacts, but we couldn't see anything because of his big head. "Look again, loser. She's into it."

"Check the chart. What's mutual masturbation get him?" Jameson reached for the scorebook we'd been keeping. He flipped to the page in the back where we'd written the rubric. "No points unless he can..." He slammed the book shut and Finn smacked the computer closed. The basement was off limits to anyone but the three of us and Keaton, so if it wasn't Keats, somebody was going to take an ass whopping. Of course, if it was Keaton—we hadn't really clued him on our video enterprise yet—the night might've still ended up with a fight.

"What are you guys doing?" Of course, it was Keaton.

Finn drummed his fingers on top of the laptop. "Nothing. Just hanging."

Keaton, probably the smartest of all of us, nodded. "I don't want to know about it." But he leaned against the wall, halfway to the door, which meant he wanted to know about it. He just didn't want to ask. And I wasn't about to tell. Keaton was too buttoned-up, too straight line to understand this year's pledge week festivities. Not that he was too buttoned up on camera. In front of the lens— whether he knew it or not, and he didn't—he sent buttons flying with regularity.

"What are you guys really doing?"

I chuckled. "Making sex videos." Nothing truthier than the truth would get him over himself.

"The three of you? Who's the lollipop?" Extra emphasis on the p's.

I stood and put my body between him and the computer. I needed to get him out of this room and put his mind on anything else. I ran through a list of names... women I could hook him up with who could distract him until the end of the week anyway.

I walked close enough I could throw an arm around his shoulders and lead him to the steps. "Do you know Beth?" I told him all about her—journalism major, gorgeous, a Sigma full of school spirit and intelligence to match her beauty. It didn't take a genius to know Keaton was tired of sorority girls and sports groupies, but Beth was extraordinary. He wanted more than a one-night stand. And I wanted him out of the way. I could pass a number along. What could it hurt?

5

Reese

et another day passed, and I still had no plan. No idea how to set Ryder free and not end up in jail. I'd had him locked in the basement for four days now, and I wasn't any closer to figuring out what to do with him. Honestly, I *wanted* to do plenty of things with him. But as his captor, it would've felt cheap and sleazy, although he had flirted yesterday and that kiss—even though it was nowhere near my lips—felt intimate and personal, made me want…him. All of him. Again. Like the pathetic fool I was.

Avery handed me a glass of wine and we sat at the table. Mom's bills were spread out in front of us, sorted—by Avery—into neat piles according to how past due they were. She took her seat and picked up the pencil to finish the tally.

After a minute, she dropped the pencil and sighed.

"How bad is it?"

By the speed at which she finished her glass and poured another, I didn't need a number to know it was going to take everything I had plus more.

"Bad." She turned the pad around and my heart stopped. "Seriously? That's…oh my God." The mountain of debt was…Everest. My cash reserve was…a knoll.

Avery sighed. "There was no life insurance?"

Life insurance? That was a funny thought. Probably not something Mom ever considered either. "She was a spiritual advisor who didn't believe in doctors or western medicine." I'd had to take money out of my retirement fund to pay for the funeral.

Avery's lips twitched and she tilted her head from one side to the other a few times. Her tell for when she wanted to say something and didn't know how.

"What?"

"Just an idea." She rubbed her hands together and sat back in the chair. "You can't yell at me, okay?" I nodded because she wouldn't finish until I agreed. Besides, she was here helping me. Any suggestion was worth considering. Especially since it came from friendship. "You should ransom Ryder."

From Insanity. "Are you out of your freaking mind?" She poured another glass of wine and sucked it down while I formulated how to continue without cursing and telling her how absolutely crazy she was. "I'm a cop, Avery. I'm sure ransoming a hostage goes against one or two rules in the handbook."

"But kidnapping is on the approved crimes list?"

Touche. "I can't ransom him." Mrs. Kennedy would have me strung up by my thumbnails and probably publicly flogged. "I wouldn't even know how." And it wasn't like there was a how-to YouTube video I could consult. "I can't." But I probably could. And it would solve two problems at once. The money. And what to do with Ryder. Of course, while I was locked up for twenty to life, still owning the only home Mom and I had would mean very little.

"Then you're going to lose the house." She picked up the most recent letter from the bank, read a few lines, then tossed it back onto the table. "In five days."

"Think I can sell it in five days?" Even I wasn't naïve enough to think that would work. Or that I could even get it cleaned up enough to sell. In a month.

"Oh yeah. And when you put the ad on Zillow, don't forget to list the basement to dungeon upgrade, the hostage in the basement, and the new rigging that allows for easy captivity." On a normal day, I appreciated her dry humor. Today was not a normal day. "Before you sell the house though, you should..." She wiggled her eyebrows and used her head to motion toward the basement door.

"I should what?" There was no way she was suggesting that I sleep with Ryder. Not that I hadn't thought about it. A couple times. Or more. But he was my...gulp...hostage. And even though, until today, he'd stopped being a pain in my ass and accepted his stay here, I couldn't...do that. "Don't be ridiculous. The harness would get in the way of the condom." It wouldn't.

She crossed her arms and smug-smiled. "So you've thought about it."

"No." She cocked her head and crossed her arms, not at all buying my blatant lies. Fine. "Okay. Maybe once or twice. Maybe last night in an x-rated dream that…" I flushed just thinking about it. "Made me want to go downstairs and repay that particular favor."

There was nothing I could get past her. "I love Keaton with all my heart, but even I noticed what that harness does for Little Ryder. You should jump on and ride that thing until the sheriff comes to enforce the eviction order."

"Don't think I haven't considered it." I had. Often. Knowing he was downstairs had made sleeping rough. When I did manage to fall asleep, I dreamed of him. I needed to figure out what to do soon, before I ended up doing him.

"You could walk away from here with a fond…fond memory."

"I have fond memories. As much as I would love to…I can't go there again." I sighed. "Besides, what if he's lost his mojo or something? It would ruin masturbation for me." I shook my head. "I can't sleep with Ryder." But as soon as she left, I was going to go into my room and pretend I was.

She rolled her eyes. "Why not? When's the last time you got fucked? And I'm not talking some two-minute fling with a guy who couldn't ring your bell with…a bell ringer. When was the last time your eyes rolled back into your head and sweat rolled down your back and somebody who looked like Ryder Kennedy made you glad you had tits and a pussy?"

"Wow. That's blunt." And personal. And depressing.

"How long?"

"A decade." She pointed to the basement, and I nodded. "Yeah."

"Then it's time."

I would've added a middle finger salute, but Ryder tapped on the ceiling and called out. "Reese!"

He'd spent most of the day crying wolf. Disturbing me as I sorted through Mom's belongings, and cleaned out the things I wouldn't be taking home with me. At least ten times he'd called me downstairs. Once he was too cold. Once to loosen the harness. Once to adjust the television because he couldn't reach it and the window put a glare on the screen. A couple times just because he was lonely and wanted to chat.

I rolled my eyes at Avery. "I'll be right back." I walked down the stairs. "What do you need?" Every time I came down the steps, I braced myself for that initial first glance of him. It knocked the wind out of me every time.

He was kicked back on the bed with his ankles and arms crossed. "I want to show you something." He pointed to the vent in the ductwork above the bed. We'd had to put it there—the bed—because we had to put the tether behind it so he could reach the important stuff without being able to get to the steps. I'd added extra blankets to the bed in case he wanted them. But I hadn't had heat or air on yet.

"What about it?" If he'd called me down here to complain because it was making his eyes dry or because it blew dust at him, I might have killed him. Instead, Avery's phone rang and I immediately understood. It only took two of Avery's sentences for me to want to die. I could hear every word she said as if she was sitting next to me. "Oh my God."

He grinned. "I was thinking…you could call me Quasimodo."

Oh, fuck.

If the world swallowed me in the very next second, it wouldn't have been soon enough. Especially when he stood and motioned to his dick. "I've been ringing bells since I was old enough to appreciate the…sound."

My skin was on fire, and I was in danger of spontaneously combusting from humiliation. "Oh, my God."

He stood and walked—stalked toward me, crooking his finger with that same old sexy smile tilting his mouth. "Let's make a memory. A fond memory." He tucked his hand into my hair and lowered his head so that his breath warmed my ear. "Also, you should definitely try to ransom me."

His voice made me want to purr, but I couldn't catch an entire breath. "You just want to go home."

"Not until you're ready for me to go." He tugged until my chest was pressed against his and our bodies lined up and I could feel his heartbeat under my hand. Then he spoke. Husky. Soft. A caress as much as his hand on my hip. "Do you want me to go?"

What the hell was I doing? The thought lasted the entire amount of time it took him to drag his lips along my jaw to my mouth. A tease. A flick of his tongue. Just enough for my panties and every working brain cell I owned to disappear. "No."

"Get rid of Avery and come back."

I nodded. "Okay."

He walked me as far as the tether would allow, then turned me again so he could wrap his arms around me. "Come back soon."

To be honest, I wasn't even concerned about Avery upstairs. If Ryder had made a move, she would've got to listen to me calling out his name a few thousand times. I ran up the stairs and picked her purse off the counter, shoved it into her arms, and pulled her from her chair. "You have to go."

"What? Why?"

"I want to make a memory. Now." I widened my eyes and pulled her toward the front entryway. "Unless you're sticking around to blog the event, you need to go.,"

"Woah, woah, wait, Horny McHornergirl." What? Didn't care. "Do you even have a box of condoms? Edible massage oil? A tickle feather? Lube?"

"A tickle feather?" I didn't need that kind of insight into her love life.

She laughed and smacked my arm. "I'm kidding. But you do need condoms. You don't know where he's been and last thing you need right now is bouncing baby Ryder."

True, but… "You are such a mood killer."

"Not nearly as much as a two-o'clock feeding or a shitty diaper and it's your turn." She swallowed hard. "I have to go." She flung the door open. "Remember, have fun, but no glove, no love." She ran to her car through a mist of rain.

One Decade Ago

Ryder

I WALKED into the frat house, smiling. Exhausted. In need of a shower and some sleep. But I'd never been happier. Never been more...in love. I should've regretted the amount of money I spent this weekend. Should've never done it. When the credit card bill came in, I was going to have to go back to my mother and beg her to take care of it for me. And by beg, there would be actual hands and knees pleading for money. Her mean streak would demand it. And then, no telling if she would come through or not.

Maybe it was time I went out and found a job. It would have to pay the big bucks and fast to make up the money I needed right now, but there had to be something. Still, I couldn't find it in my guts to be sorry I'd spent the money on Reese this weekend. Couldn't regret one second of the time we'd spent at the hotel. Or the plane tickets to surprise her. Or the bottle of champagne and room service lobster. Worth every penny and every second of degrading Mom would hand out when she got the bill. Nothing was going to ruin my day. Not even the decibel level at the frat house.

There were brothers everywhere. Drinking in front of a set of screens playing every game and race known to man. Shooting pool. Throwing darts. Arguing over which *Sports Illustrated* model filled out her swimsuit better. And none of it was getting on my nerves the way it normally did.

I walked through the house whistling a happy tune.

Hell, I didn't even know I could whistle. Finn and Keaton were in the game room, talking smack while they monopolized one of the big screens and a video game console. I needed to check this weekend's video action, but right now I wanted to sit with my buddies and hear about their weekend. Plus, Reese wanted me to ask Keaton and Susie to double with us to a concert she'd won four tickets to see.

It had been a couple weeks since I set Keats up with Beth. He'd sealed the deal a couple times, but I wasn't sure if he was still seeing her since I'd been away all weekend. With Reese. In Boston. A penthouse suite we never left.

I slapped him on the back as I plopped onto the sofa next to him. He glanced at me then immediately back to the screen. "Your old man dropped off some money for you today. He put it in your room."

Good old Dad. Sneaking some extra funding past Mom. And thank God because my cash supply was dwindling. Two nights in the penthouse suite was more than Mom gave me in three months. And that was before room service. The tips took all my available cash and a couple advances on my card. I'd spent a lot more than Dad would be able to sneak past her. I needed a plan and fast. "You know where Jay is?" He'd mentioned something a while back. Something I would need help setting up. Something that had to remain top secret.

"Downstairs, I think," Finn answered, wiggling his eyebrows as Keaton's on-screen avatar shot a missile and blew Finn's avatar to video game hell. He started another game.

Good. I needed them distracted. I needed them not to

overhear. I needed money desperately and they'd never go for this. Never let me use the pledges so blatantly or—probably—illegally. I diminished the guilt with a breath. Lying to them would suck. Thank God, it was only for a little while.

I walked down the steps, not quietly, but not announcing my presence either. Jameson had one screen tuned to the boat, and one playing back an earlier video. He had both hands on the desk though, so I wasn't worried I'd caught him doing anything. Not until he slammed the laptop closed.

"Whatcha looking at, buddy?" I sounded as if I'd taken up singing in my spare time. Like I needed every sentence to have its own melody. It had to be the happiness making me so ridiculous.

"Nothing. Just…a video. One of the pledges." His skin pinked all the way to the tips of his ears.

"Anything good?"

"No. Not really. I thought you were in Boston." He unplugged his laptop from the server and tucked it under his arm then stood. Apparently, we were walking back upstairs if I wanted to talk to him.

"Just got back." And while I really wanted to see what was on his computer that he so badly didn't want me to see, I needed his help, and embarrassing him wouldn't entice him to keep my secrets. "And I was thinking about starting my own business. And I need a really good computer guy. Somebody discreet." I lifted my eyebrows hoping I was communicating a message I hadn't yet found voice to speak.

He grinned. "Some 007 shit?"

Thank God for Jameson King. "Better."

And it only took a couple days before we were up and running and the money started pouring in. I was never going to have to beg my mother for money again. I'd found my gold mine.

6

Ryder

I was helping the woman who kidnapped me. Who tased me. Who strapped me into a harness and attached me to her wall. Not only was I helping her. I wanted her. Wanted to kiss her. Everywhere. And then I wanted to slide my hands over her skin, slowly, until we were both burning with need, aching, desperate. Then I wanted to cover her body with mine, let my cock...

"Hey." She walked to the bed, in the same clothes she'd been wearing earlier. Not that I'd expected lingerie or even something without the streak of dust across the front, because in no way was I turning anything down when it came to Reese, but had I not been harnessed into my clothes, I would've put on a clean shirt.

"You okay?" The tight, constipated look was a red flag.

"Yeah. But we should talk."

In the history of men and women, since Adam and Eve,

no man ever wanted to hear those words. I was no different. I wanted to fuck. Talk was only going to get in the way of that.

"Okay." I moved to sit beside her and kept my hands in my lap. "What's up?" I'd been thinking about her, naked and underneath me for the last hour and a half. I already knew what was up. Kept it to myself in the interest of still having a chance with her and waited.

She blew out a breath, wiped her palms together, folded her hands then tapped her thumbs. I leaned closer to sniff her. We all had our nervous habits.

"I want you." Although, her strained voice sounded anything but horny.

I smiled. "Good. I want you, too."

"But we can't."

I nodded like I agreed then stopped, looked at her once, then again. "Wait, what?"

"I kidnapped you."

I chuckled then covered with a cough when her eyes narrowed. "I didn't think it would be a turn-on, but...it is." Apparently, she didn't agree. "Seriously. It's hot." This was my chance. "And that hasn't happened for me in a while."

"Oh, well how long has it been since someone tased you, threw you in a trunk, and cuffed you to a bed?"

Distraction was my only hope. And I needed hope. I needed her. And I wasn't about to give up over a couple of cold feet and some second thoughts. "Happens more often than you'd think." She huffed and turned toward the TV. I clicked the remote and cupped her cheek with my free hand so she had to look at me. "It doesn't have to be more than what it is."

"And what is it?" Her soft voice touched a string in my heart and I wanted to tell her how I'd never forgotten her, how sorry I was she got hurt, and that I had any part in that, how much she'd meant to me then. And now.

Instead, I smiled and lied. "It's one night. An itch we're going to scratch that doesn't mean you're writing my name in heart bubbles with those little eyes and the lashes." I'd found the paper in a notebook I'd borrowed to copy notes from. And at the memory, she turned as dark crimson as I'd ever seen her.

"That was ten years ago."

I grinned. "I kept the paper. Had it framed."

There was nothing sexier in the world than her laugh. Except her laugh when she was naked. Hopefully, we'd get there soon.

"That's okay. I have eighty copies." She tilted her chin to look at me. "You're welcome to another one if you want."

"Thanks." I waited. A range of emotions played across her face—fear, courage, desire. In the end, desire won and she leaned in, curled her fingers into the front of my shirt, and pulled me closer.

Just as we were about to make contact, she pulled the brake. "Wait." Instead of leaving or moving, she tucked her hand into her pocket and produced the key to the lock that secured the harness. As soon as she sprung the lock, she pulled the straps away and I stepped free. I'd been trussed up for days and being able to move, to have a full range of motion, was almost as intoxicating as Reese.

She smiled and moved in again. I slid my arm around her and moved until the backs of her knees hit the edge of the mattress. I laid her down then moved next to her. The first kiss was a freefall. A whole body experience. Her lips parted and her tongue slid against mine. One of her hands tangled in my hair and the other twisted in my shirt. She threw her leg over my hip and hauled my cock closer to her pussy.

White hot desire surged through me. The intensity would send her running, so I let her take control. She rolled me onto my back and climbed on top, one leg on each side of my hips. I held her, arms straining against the desire to crush her against me. Instead, I trailed a finger up her spine under her shirt and she broke the kiss to fling it away.

I couldn't stop looking at her. The perfection of her curves, the smooth, supple skin, the raw sensuality. Nothing gentle or hesitant. And if she'd been beautiful before—and she was—now she was exquisite. And powerful.

Once I started, really started, there was no way I would ever want to stop. And that scared me enough that I faltered, lost focus.

And she noticed. "Just scratching an itch, right?"

I nodded and kissed her again, sat up, and held her to me before I relaxed and settled in enough to cup her breast, enjoy the weight of it in my hand before I lowered my head and caught her nipple in my mouth. Nothing tasted as good as her skin. I moaned when she held my head against her. To know that she was into it made me even hotter and

I wanted control of the moment. I wanted to make up for lost years. For wasted time.

Nothing meant more to me than making her happy. She arched her back in my hands and I kissed the valley between her breasts before I moved to the other nipple. I wanted to kiss her from throat to ankle, and I had a few spots I wanted to spend some time exploring, getting to know her again, but I wasn't going to last long.

"I haven't done this in a while." Nor had I intended to blurt that out.

"So you said." She lifted my shirt. "It's okay. I've taken care of myself before."

Not with me. And not helpful to my situation. "Woman." But she was gone. Sliding down my body. Taking my nipple between her teeth, twisting until I sucked in a breath, then she let go and the relief sent blood straight to my dick. And she was still moving down. Her tongue traced my muscles while her hand found my cock, then lower and back again to my shaft. She squeezed gently then stroked and when she wrapped her lips around me and sucked me deep into her throat, I groaned and closed my eyes.

"Watch me." Her words registered but I couldn't do more than lie there and feel. "Watch me suck your dick, Ryder." I looked down my body, and she stroked my cock with her hand and then her mouth.

"Fuck, Reese."

And by fuck I meant, holy fuck. I remembered the night we'd met—watching her in the back of my Escalade—for just a second before I lost all thought whatsoever and every muscle went tight. "Oh, God, Reese." I tried to pull her away, but she hung on, sucked harder, took me deeper until I exploded in her throat, and still, she worked me until she had every last drop and I couldn't do more than breathe.

I unfisted the sheet and knew it was going to be a few minutes before I could bounce back—I wasn't twenty-three anymore—and she deserved...everything. "My turn."

"You don't have to."

I chuckled and nodded, kissing her nipple, swirling my tongue in a way that made her moan and bite her lip. When I moved down and nipped her stomach, she gasped. When I did it a second time, she moaned. And when I nipped lower, she whimpered until I finally swiped my tongue over her clit and slid a finger inside her. She writhed and I held her.

She was tight and wet and ready and I wanted every-thing she had to give but first I wanted this. To hear all those little sounds of ecstasy.

"Ryder, God. Please." And to hear her say my name.

Every sound she made, every muscle she flexed, every twist of her body made me want her all over again, but when her body went rigid and her legs tightened around me, she cried out.

I lifted my head and moved to lie beside her, to circle her nipple with my finger and to kiss a line along her collar bone. "Please, what, Reese?"

"Please, fuck me."

Enough said.

One Decade Ago

Reese

"WHERE ARE WE GOING?" Never mind I was blindfolded in a car whose destination I didn't know. Also, never mind we'd already had two bottles—maybe two and a half—of champagne, and I was a little too tipsy for a late night jaunt across campus without more than his hand and a few words of encouragement to guide me.

"Almost there." He slowed our stroll and leaned in to kiss me.

And it was enough to shut me up and convince me to walk on. At least, until we stopped at our destination. A backyard. Not just any backyard, but one with a blanket spread on the ground, a pile of pillows, and more wine behind a house big enough my family home would've fit in three times with room to spare. Three stories of brick and mortar broken by three stories of floor to ceiling windows and all of them looking out at us. At least in the part I could see. Four sets of glass double doors opened onto a stone patio with thick-cushioned furniture. Our blanket shared space with a swimming pool, a tennis court down a big hill, and a putting green.

"What are we doing?"

He pulled me down beside him on the blanket, took my face in his hands, and kissed me so softly I thought I might melt. "This is where I live when we're not at school." And my mind turned this very romantic thing into something bad. I was good enough to be introduced to his backyard, but not to his family. I stood and yanked my hand out of his. "What's wrong?" His forehead narrowed toward his scalp and he frowned, tried to take my hand again, and tilted his head when I pulled away.

"I don't know." Oh, but I did know. I could feel how wrong it was in every fiber of my being. But I started walking back as if I had any clue how to get around the monstrosity of flowerbeds and giant pool house, stone privacy fence—I chose the wrong way. Every step, every second, my guts twisted more, and the anger seeped through. He was using me. Obviously, I wasn't the normal college co-ed. I didn't wear make-up. Or spew my school spirit on any passerby. But I was a person he hung out with, sometimes fully clothed. But I wasn't good enough to introduce to his family. He was ashamed of me.

I didn't realize I was muttering until he took my arm. When I jerked hard enough I punched myself in the chest, I shot him a glare and gritted my teeth. "I want to go home." And that part of me was at war with the part that wanted the white-hot, melt steel minutes I was passing up with my temper tantrum.

He held up his hands. "Okay." I walked a few steps because being so near him broke the spot inside of me I was holding together. "Reese, it's this way." I turned and stared for a second before walking back.

We hadn't made it around the side of the yard when security lights flipped on and a woman, one who spent a lot on hair and makeup because even the slight wind didn't move her perfect coif and I doubted she'd been primping inside waiting to catch us in the yard, walked out from the patio doors. "William! I don't know how many times I've told you not to bring your whores..." She stopped short when she saw us. "Ryder."

No apology. Just steel. Ice. Venom. Her voice had it all. In one word. That was some admirable power. And it didn't let up when whoever William was turned out to be Ryder.

"Mom. This is Reese."

She barely spared me a glance. Not that I wanted the eye of Sauron on me without a hobbit for protection. Instead, she glared at Ryder. "Your father has your grades. Lucky for you, he hasn't shown them to me yet." Her tone wasn't angry. More disappointed. At least wanting him to think she was disappointed. It was a tone my mom used when she tried to trick me into telling her the truth. I was immune. Ryder, not so much.

He looked down at his shoes. "They're good this semester, Mom. I've been studying. Reese and I—"

Her scoff was as loud as the sound of Ryder swallowing. "And now you're bringing your little..." She gave me an up-and-down look that burned me with her distaste. "Friends home." She shot me a glare. "I don't know what he's told you, but he has nothing, not a dime until he graduates from college and passes the bar exam. And should this relationship last..." she cocked an eyebrow that said she had her doubts, and I didn't speak because I felt Ryder dying beside me, and I didn't want to make it worse for him. "You'll be expected to sign a prenup." Before I could tell her to kiss my ass, she turned and stormed into her house.

"I'm so sorry, Reese." He shoved his hands in his pockets and kept his chin down.

My heart broke for a brand new reason, and all I wanted was to see his smile. And if it made me pathetic, then I was pathetic. "I think your mom and I made a real connection."

He smiled and pulled me close. "It's not you I'm ashamed of." Then he lowered his head and kissed me. Soft and slow. Then hard and deep. Consuming. One hand in my hair the other on my hip. Tongue sliding against mine as he pushed me against the side of the house. The brick was rough and cold, but heat burned inside of me, and I loved the way his body pressed into mine, aligned in the best spots. I could feel all the ridges and planes of his stomach and legs and every single space in between.

I wanted him. But that was nothing new. I could deny it when we weren't together, but when we were in the same place, desire vibrated through me and I was weak for him. "Ryder..."

He pulled back breathing hard, forehead against mine. "You are too much to resist." The need in his voice, the tremble in the hand he slid under the hem of my shirt just below my ribs, and the shallow, short breaths, mirrored everything I felt. "Stay with me tonight." And as if I didn't understand his meaning, he added, "All night."

"Here?" Seeing his mom again might have been the one thing powerful enough to put the kibosh on my desire.

He laughed. "God, no. You can stay at the frat house with me."

Oh, hell no. "Or there's a nice bench in that little bus

stop shelter on Main street in front of the diner." And God, I loved his laugh. Loved it more when I earned it with a joke, which wasn't the case at that moment. No way was I staying at the frat house with all of his frat friends and their frat beers and thin frat walls. "We could just stay at my place." Beth wouldn't care. She had plenty of overnight guests who apparently inspired her middle-of-the-night prayers.

"Beth hates me." True. And maybe not a strong enough verb for what she felt. "Please stay with me." And he kissed me again and again until I didn't care anymore about anything besides waking up beside him in the morning.

7

Reese

Ten years disappeared in a blink. The time apart never happened. And here I was lying next to him, head on his chest, arm over his stomach like I'd always been here.

Ryder stroked my arm and kissed the top of my head. "Who would've thought?" The blanket smelled like him. I'd never be able to walk in this basement again and not see him. Fortunately, I wasn't going to be able to afford to own the basement for much longer so seeing him wherever I looked wouldn't be a problem.

I smiled because it was easy to smile while I was lying beside him with no worries about the world on my shoulders. "I certainly never dreamed when I kidnapped you that I'd end up…here."

"Really?" He sighed. "My ego was all big and full,

thinking you brought me here to make me your love slave." Oh, the thought. "I mean, I wished anyway."

The Ryder I'd known in college was confident to the point of almost cockiness. He was self-assured. Never humble. Seeing his vulnerability now made me wish we didn't have the history we had. I wanted to make him feel better. To build him back up into the boy I'd fallen so hard for.

Instead, I snuggled closer, savoring this because the future, ours, mine, the future of our relationship, was uncertain. His arms tightened around me and neither of us spoke for a few minutes. "What are you going to do about the house?"

"You know, we almost didn't stay here. If it wasn't for your mom..." I knew he didn't want to hear it. "When she hired my mom as her advisor, it changed everything for us."

"Yeah."

"This was the first place my mom ever hung a picture. Or bought a lamp. Isn't that..." Strange. A weird family fact. But one that made letting go of this place harder than I thought it would be. But the fact was, I didn't live here anymore. I didn't have a reason to keep it. And Glouster wasn't really a vacation home kind of place. Not that I had a job that allowed me to afford a vacation home.

"I never asked where you live now."

"I live in California." Might as well have been the other side of the world. "And I have to go back soon."

He nodded. "I figured."

"So it just makes sense to let the house go." My heart

ached. "I have a couple days left to pack it up. I can ship some stuff home and the rest I'll donate or have hauled away."

"Sounds like you have a plan."

Not a good one. Normally, I loved California. The sun. The palm trees. The beach. The work. I didn't live in LA. I lived in a small wealthy town. Worked in LA, but I was a detective. Had a desk and a good partner. But today all I wanted was winter and snow, to watch the sun come up over the ocean. To snuggle in front of the fireplace. With Ryder.

"Yeah. A plan."

He sat higher in the bed, his back against the headboard, and I moved with him so we were sitting next to each other, shoulder to shoulder now. I took a moment to fawn over him before I smiled.

"Or you could still ransom me. You could get the money to keep the house and stay in it when you come back to visit."

I wouldn't be able to come back. Not often enough to sustain any kind of relationship. Although this one night was more of a relationship than I'd had since the first time I dated him. It at least involved conversation outside of *your place or mine.*

"What if your mom calls the cops? I could lose everything." As someone who had been through that kind of loss, I would've thought he'd understand.

"Okay. What if I…" He shook his head. "I could ask my dad for the money. He's always offering to give me cash."

"I wouldn't be able to pay it back. I live pretty close to

the vest as it is." California's cost of living was ridiculous, and cops weren't the best-paid Californians.

"Then I'll buy the house and you'll always have a place to come back to." He swallowed and took me by the shoulders, turning us to face each other. "What I'm saying is, this wasn't just scratching an itch for me."

Fuck. I couldn't do this again. Our history was too complicated, too hurtful. Plus, once a cheater, always a cheater. I pulled out of his hold and turned to stand and pull on my shirt. It was draped over the TV where I'd tossed it hours ago. And I concentrated on slipping it over my head to give myself a minute. I was going to say something so hurtful, so untrue, but so necessary, and I needed a breath first.

I yanked on my panties and looked at him. "It was for me."

And if he decided to call the police and tell them I kidnapped him, then fine. It was what it was. I would be upstairs waiting and packing.

One Decade Ago

BETH BURST INTO MY ROOM. It was the first night I'd spent away from Ryder in a while, but he'd had to go home, and I needed some sleep. Hence the reason I threw a pillow at Beth. "Get out."

"You have to get up now. Something big is going down." There was a note of alarm in her voice and it sent a shiver down my spine.

I burrowed under my blanket to escape the cold already in my bones. "I don't care."

She tugged my arm, then gave up when I jerked away. A second later, she was back with her iPad. "Did he take any videos of you?"

"What?" Videos? Of me? Who? I could only think in very small questions.

"Did you let Ryder video you two having sex?" She pulled up a website and turned the screen to face me. In living color, there were GIFs of Keaton with…six different girls, Finn with…Oh, God. Ryder. I searched the GIFs on the front page. No Ryder. Second page. No Ryder. But then…on page three.

My stomach clenched. My heart stopped. My guts ached. Ryder. I didn't need to see more. But I couldn't stop looking. This was my train wreck.

"What the fuck is this?"

Beth shook her head. "It's all over campus. The Alphas have been using their boat to film themselves with women and charging for views. I have to go. I need to get the story, but…I thought you should know."

Nothing like a good morning heart attack to get one to sit straight up in bed. I clicked on a GIF—not one of Ryder, but of Keaton—and watched for a second. Neither one of them seemed particularly aware they were being filmed. That was to say they weren't playing to the camera. Weren't concerned with good sides or lighting or whether the camera saw too much or too little or about what it heard.

I searched through the GIFs. There were none of me. Thank God.

"Who knows about this?" I threw back the blankets. I had to get to Ryder. I didn't hear her answer as I popped into the bathroom that connected our rooms. When I came back out, she was watching a video on her tablet. I could hear the moaning. "Who knows about it?" I asked her again then snapped my fingers in front of her as I slipped a shoe on.

"Everybody, I think." She clicked the off button so my room went quiet. "I'm on my way to a protest outside the Alpha house right now." She laughed. "You know Susie, right? The one who's been trying to gather girls to paint the frat house every night? Well..." She launched into a story my brain was too addled to comprehend all of, but the gist was Susie had slept with one of the Alphas, got dumped, and got angry. Decided to take her rage out on the front of the frat house. Every day she painted a new dirty word on the front and every day they had the pledges clean it off. "She's got all the girls she could find standing outside the Alpha house right now."

"I have to get over there." Ryder had to be innocent, right? I ignored the fact—for now—that he had videos on the site that weren't with me. We hadn't talked about being monogamous. Although we spent so much time together I just assumed we weren't seeing anyone but each other.

"Reese..." When I ignored her, she took one of my shoulders in each of her hands and gave me a little shake. "They suspended all four of them. Said Ryder..." She looked down at the floor. I wanted to hurt her. Hurt him. Hurt everyone.

"Said Ryder did what?" It was better to know than not to know.

She blew a long breath from her puffy cheeks. "They said Ryder is the one who…did it all. That he was the mastermind, anyway, but they're all suspended."

I stared at her. Suspended. Ryder. His mom would kill him. I had to get to him. There had to be a way to prove he was innocent. If. If he was innocent.

"Come on." I pulled her by the arm this time until she stood. "I need to go there."

And if I needed help burying the body, so to speak, she would be there for me.

She chattered the entire time she drove across town and didn't close her mouth until we pulled onto the street behind the Alpha House. The front of the house was full of picketers and the back was surrounded by the fence, but I would rather take my chances climbing the fence than with a bunch of enraged victims of whatever was going on.

"I'm going to pull the car as close to the fence as I can so we can use it to climb over." It was a Mercedes convertible. Not much in the help department. But it also didn't have enough room to bring a ladder, so any help was better than none.

"Okay."

I climbed over first and waited for her at the bottom before I weaved through the beer cans, the firepits, assorted debris, and mismatched chairs and furniture in the yard between me and the back door. It opened into the kitchen which usually smelled like old cheese, stale beer, and hot wing sauce, but today smelled fresh and clean and every surface sparkled.

The whole house was dust-free and dazzling. Candle scented. Empty. I walked around another corner to the staircase that led to Ryder's room. The silence was loud, broken only by the tick of the grandfather clock in the foyer and our shoes on the polished tile floor.

"Jesus, Reese. This place gives me the creeps."

I nodded because I agreed. With my whole heart.

The steps had a red paisley carpet that followed to a matching runner at the top that went both ways down the hallway. "His room's this way." I went to the end of the hall. It was a big room. Twice the size of mine, although mine had more space because I had way less stuff. No stereo system or weight bench. No sound-mixing or movie-making equipment.

Movie. Making. Equipment.

Shit.

But the desk was empty. The computer and all its attachments missing.

I circled the bed, looking for...I didn't know what. For something that would prove him innocent, although I didn't have any idea what it would be.

The room smelled like him. Had the clothes I'd folded for him still sitting in a chair. "Where're they all at?"

I shook my head. "I have no idea." But every fiber in my body said the answer wasn't a good one.

8

Ryder

Two days ago, leaving here was the only thing I wanted. This morning, the walk up the stairs was one of the hardest of my life. It was going to make going back to my apartment nearly impossible, especially knowing she was here.

I came out of the basement and stopped to watch her. She was at the table in the kitchen, fingers curled around a coffee mug, hair pulled up, clothes fresh, house scented by her bath soap. The rain from yesterday hadn't quite finished yet and provided the soundtrack for today through the open window.

"Hey." I couldn't just stand there staring at her. I had to say something.

She didn't turn so I couldn't see her face but her voice cracked. "Are you leaving now?"

I didn't want to. And she hadn't exactly asked me to

leave. "Not if you want me to stay. That ransom thing could work." *Say it.* I moved closer, my hand hovering over her shoulder because I wanted to touch her. Nothing sexual. Just to touch her was enough. But she'd pulled the brakes. Hence, the hovering.

"No. It's okay."

I shoved the hovering hand into my pocket. "Thanks for washing my clothes."

"Least I could do." She shrugged. "Seriously. Very least."

I wasn't going to get anywhere, wouldn't be able to change her mind, and I couldn't blame her. "I'll see you later?" The old me wouldn't have put a question mark at the end. He would have helped her up from her chair then kissed her until we ended up in bed again. Fuck. I missed that guy.

She cleared her throat. "I'm probably going to fly home tomorrow or the next day."

Not what I wanted to hear. "Reese…" Yeah. I was going to ask her to stay. To beg. To offer her…nothing. Because I had nothing.

"It's been great catching up."

Catching up? We were calling it *catching up?* The hell we were. "Reese." She remained focused on whatever she'd found more interesting outside the window. I breathed out, slow, loud, a decision-making breath. "I could go for some more catching up."

Suddenly the window wasn't the most interesting thing anymore, and she turned to look at me. "I'm still leaving in a couple days."

I shrugged like I wasn't the biggest liar in the world,

and this wasn't the most important conversation in my life. "I'm not asking you to stay." I'd already done that, and it hadn't worked. What I hadn't done was enough convincing. Yet.

"What are you asking?" She chewed the corner of her lower lip and smiled. She knew what I wanted. She just wanted to hear me say it.

I crooked my finger because once upon a time, she saw some actor do it on TV and she told me it was so sexy. Funny, the things I remembered. "Come here."

She stared at me. Passion. Desire. Need. We had it all. And now I had her standing in front of me, the hint of a smile as sexy as a full-on smile, and she laid one hand flat on my shoulder and put the other over my heart. "Is my bedroom okay?"

The counter, the floor, the kitchen table. "Yeah. That's fine." But we weren't going anywhere until I kissed her again. It was already at least an hour since the last time I kissed her and every minute that ticked away was another one wasted, one where I hadn't kissed the girl. And I was definitely the guy meant to kiss this girl. Fate demanded it. She'd come back. Kidnapped me. Made me remember what it was like to be someone who was seen.

The kiss was sexy and slow, then she opened her mouth and the whole thing evolved. Spun us through time to when we were younger and carefree, when kissing each other was the only important thing in the world.

Her lips were soft, smooth, and tasted like caramel. Her fingers tangled in my hair, strong, tugging and holding me close, so fucking close.

I lifted her, and she wrapped her legs around my hips, aligned the white heat of her body with the ever-hardening length of my cock. I couldn't get enough of the taste of her or the feel of her body in my arms. I moaned. Or maybe it was her. Or maybe it was us. Didn't matter.

We didn't make it to the bedroom. We made it to the wall. She pushed my jeans down. I shoved her sweats away and she kicked them off. Then, she kissed me again. Harder, hotter. And my blood burned, the world spiraled away. It was me and Reese, and nothing else mattered.

I held her up with my hips as she lowered onto my dick. Slick and hot, frenzied and desperate. Pants around my ankles and shirts pushed out of the way. It was a total loss of control. Like we hadn't just spent an entire night rolling around the bed in the basement. Made use of the hand-cuffs, licked whipped cream off each other...and now, again, I was buried inside her, impatient to hear her call out my name, beg me to never stop.

Driven by need, I bucked my hips, and she clutched my shoulders, her nails biting into my skin. Her legs tightened, and she shuddered. Cried out, whimpered, cried out again. The sound, the feel of her, the kiss I couldn't resist when her lips parted again, all worked together until the pressure inside me exploded.

"Reese." I breathed her name on a moan, and she lowered her head to my shoulder and kissed my throat.

The front door opened and Felicity breezed in. Reese yanked her shirt down and dove over the back of the sofa taking a knitted afghan with her. I yanked my jeans up, but not quick enough, and thought a second too late to turn.

"Wow."

Reese lifted her head and looked at Felicity. "What?"

Felicity stopped staring at me and picked up Reese's discarded sweats and tossed them to her. "I meant, wow, it's barely ten and you guys are full on fifty shades of doing it in the living room."

Reese scowled, her recovery quicker than mine. "What are you doing here?"

"I came over because Avery said you need help taking ransom pictures. She's on her way. With a camera." Felicity smiled at me. "What were you guys doing?" No doubt she'd seen enough to know exactly what we'd been doing. This was just too much fun for her to pass up.

Reese cleared her throat. "I was just telling…um…" She gestured to me and Felicity chuckled.

"Ryder?" She smirked.

Reese glared, and I stood there dumbfounded. "I know his name. I was just telling *Ryder*"—she glanced at me, and I gave a little nod because what else was I going to do—"thank you for being a good sport."

"Yeah. Sometimes I thank Finn that way, too." Her head bobbled from shoulder to shoulder. "I don't usually thank him in the living room with the front door unlocked."

Reese's face reddened and I wanted to help her, but… "Technically, it's the kitchen wall."

Reese threw her hands up and growled. She stomped into the kitchen, opened then slammed the refrigerator door, and walked back to face Felicity. "Ransom pictures? Camera? What?"

"She said you talked about it." Felicity shrugged. "And

Finn said if you need Ryder roughed up a little bit for authenticity, he'd be happy to help." Now she aimed her smirk at me.

"I'm sure he did." But that wasn't really the point. "Reese changed her mind about ransoming me."

"I'm a cop." She shook her head.

"Maybe you should get that printed on a t-shirt. Then you could stop reminding us every ten minutes." I'd never watched Reese interact with her friends before. It reminded me of the days when I had friends of my own. The teasing. The laughing. I missed it.

Reese rolled her eyes at Felicity. "That training was really hard."

"And we can all see how you like hard things." She nodded toward me. "Were you guys at least finished? Do you need another minute?"

I glanced from the still scowling Reese—even annoyance looked good on her—to her friend. "I think we're okay."

Avery opened the door and walked in to stand beside Felicity. No one spoke, but Felicity still wore her smirk, we could've still fried eggs on Reese, and I just wanted this minute to be over. "What'd I miss?"

"I caught them."

Avery looked at her, confused, then at me and at Reese, before her mouth dropped open. "You mean…?"

Felicity nodded. "Yup. They were adding a chapter to their sex story."

Reese blew out a loud breath that was half suppressed scream, half angry growl. "We were scratching an itch.

Now we're finished and he's leaving. Can we please stop talking about it?"

If nothing else, her outburst silenced her friends until Avery recovered. "He's leaving? What happened to ransom?"

"She's a cop." This time Felicity said it.

Avery sighed and Felicity nodded as if they'd managed to exchange some subliminal message. After a moment, she glanced at Reese. "Well, if we aren't going to ransom the love king"—she jerked her thumb at me, and I gave a little wave because it just felt right—"then are we packing or... do you have some secret stash of cash you wanna tell us about?"

Reese spoke and had sadness not dripped from her every word, I would've chimed in with support for the idea of her staying, but I couldn't pile it on. "I live in California. I can't justify keeping this house."

Felicity puffed out her lower lip. "You don't have to go back to California. We have cops here, too." She ignored Reese's huff. "I'm just saying. If you wanted to hang around..." She shrugged. "We...your friends...would like that."

She looked at me, and I held up both hands because no way was I going to pressure her. Not yet, anyway. "Don't look at me. I'm just an itch." Didn't feel as nonchalant to say as I meant for my attitude to convey.

But Reese stared at me. Angry at first then she tilted her head and the gaze softened. "I think I still need a good scratch."

I couldn't look away. She didn't look away.

"I don't get this metaphor."

Avery pulled Felicity to the door. "Come on. I'll explain it over margaritas at The Rundown." The bar I should've been serving this evening.

Reese glanced away. "Hey, Avery, leave the camera?"

Avery's mouth dropped open. "Are you serious? Did you learn nothing from the love king's little video operation? I know it's been ten years since that whole mess, but—"

Reese sighed, and I tried not to take offense since I'd done all the evil they'd accused me of. Well, almost.

"It's for the ransom pictures." She winked at me, and all was right with the world once again.

One Decade Ago

Shit. There was something wrong. A glitch. A spike in payments to my account. Not that I minded the extra money. But I'd had videos of the pledges up for weeks. And I'd made some quick cash, but nothing like the deposits of the last three days.

I had about six hundred emails since midnight to the video account showing today's views along with credits to the amount of money I had. That meant the traffic to my site had increased by about five hundred views today alone. At six dollars a view, I took a pay raise of three grand. Today. And eighteen hundred each yesterday and the day before. I hadn't advertised the site. Or added to it.

Or...made a single change that would account for this increase.

There had to be a reason. I dialed Jameson. "Yo." His typical answer.

"Did you tell anybody about the site?"

He chuckled. "Hell, no. You sink or swim on this one yourself." Why I expected help from him I couldn't imagine. He wasn't exactly known for his loyalty or his willingness to pitch in if it didn't benefit him.

My phone beeped, but I didn't smile when Reese's picture showed up. I had to get home. Get those videos down because my gut said this was the beginning of something that was going to bite my ass hard.

I ended the call with Jameson and shut the whole damned phone off. I couldn't afford the distraction. Not now. I had to focus on what to do. Delete the videos. Shut down the site.

I turned onto Fraternity Road and stopped. There wasn't one cop car in front of the Alpha house. There were four along with a white van. A couple of campus security guys sat under the maple tree that needed a trim with their golf carts, barricades, and yellow tape. Beth Cooper stood on the sidewalk, a camera guy with his equipment aimed at her as she spoke into a microphone and motioned to the frat house behind her.

I didn't put any of it together. Not when I parked behind one of the cop cars. Not when two cops followed me to the porch, wouldn't let me pass, then asked if I was Ryder Kennedy. I got the distinct impression it wasn't good to be Ryder Kennedy at that moment, but I nodded anyway. And that was the moment it all became clear.

One of the cops called out, and a guy in a suit turned. "We got him."

Got him? I was *him*? "What the fuck is going on?"

Chancellor Fields came out of the house with Keaton, who shot me a glare, and Finn who gave me an almost imperceptible shake of his head.

"You need to come with us, son." The guy in the suit dug his fingers into my biceps, and I yanked away.

"I'm not going anywhere." Whatever the fuck was going on, I had more important things to deal with.

He shoved me against the wall next to the door, face to brick, and pulled my hand behind my back. I tried twisting away, but he shoved his forearm into the back of my neck and jerked my wrist toward my shoulder blades. Pain radiated up and down my spine, across my back. "Always has to be one of you little assholes who wants to do it the hard way." He muttered the words at the side of my face, his coffee breath as insulting as the insinuation I was an asshole.

"Fuck you. I haven't done anything wrong." And right then, I believed it.

And my belief lasted all of an hour because that was how long I sat in the room alone before the detective walked in. Detective Vanessa Palmer. Brown hair. Blue eyes. Slow southern accent. "Ryder Kennedy?" It came out sounding like Ride-a Kenne-day.

I nodded and smiled. Nothing smarmy. Friendly. I needed to read the room before I decided how to play her.

She flipped open a file folder. Sorted through screen-shots. A lot of screenshots. Keaton. Finn. Even Jameson. And me? Was that…no. It couldn't be. Sure as hell looked like me with Susie Chastain. But I hadn't… oh, shit. "You have been a very busy boy." Her smug look said my right to remain silent wasn't going to be enough.

"I want a lawyer." But she knew that already.

"Oh." She closed the folder and nodded. "Okay. Law student. I should've known." Instead of standing and walking out, she shuffled the photos, straightened them, folded her hands on top of the folder, and stared at me. "I hope he's a good lawyer because a boy as pretty as you is going to be very popular in jail."

"Am I under arrest?" I wasn't sure who she thought she was dealing with, but even if I wasn't prelaw, which I was, I was the son of an attorney. I knew my rights. I also knew she could hold me and the guys for twenty-four hours before she leveled a single charge against us or had to let us go.

"Why, no. We just want to have a little chat." She smiled. "Same chat my colleagues are having with your fraternity brothers." The warmth she was trying for was anything but warm and a cold shiver slipped up my spine. "I hear you boys are the cream of this year's university crop. Football stars. Academic wonder boys. And so popular with the ladies."

If she didn't stop, she was going to blow whatever it was she was trying to do. "I asked for a lawyer."

"I know. We'll get to that. But I'm not questioning you, Mr. Kennedy. Just talking while we wait." Sinister talking, maybe. The kind wrapped in evil intentions. The kind I was way too smart to get tangled up in. "So, let me tell you what I think happened." I cocked an eyebrow, and she smiled. My guts were in knots. But I waited for her to continue. "I think you and your friends have had quite the schoolyear so far. A lot of dates. And no denying, you all are nice looking. Very handsome. But getting to know you, it makes me wonder about women." She shook her head. "Anyway. Did you get the dates for them or was this as spontaneous as it looks on video?" She covered her mouth. "Oops. That was a question, wasn't it?" A fake, forced giggle erupted. "I think you tricked those girls, or you lied to them, or you just plain old didn't tell them. Either way, unless you can produce some evidence that you had permission to make videos of these ladies being intimate with your friends, I'm going to assume, they didn't know, and I'm going to put you and your friends in jail for invading their privacy, for exploitation, for solicitation. So many crimes. So many girls." Her smile was like maple syrup, sticky, too sweet.

I stared at her, trying to keep my face blank, but she was right. I was way too pretty for jail. "Lawyer."

She stood and nodded. "All right, Mr. Kennedy. I'll get someone to help you with that. In the meantime, I'm going to go have a little powwow with your friends. See if any of them want to make a deal."

What the fuck? She hadn't offered me a deal. "A deal?"

She nodded. "Yes. I think whichever one of them turns on you first is going to become my favorite fraternity boy. But if they all want to testify you were the mastermind, I can probably work something out for each one." She winked and walked to the door. "I'm gonna get you that phone call now."

Surely, my friends wouldn't…they didn't know anything. Only Jameson. But one of them had to have uploaded the videos. So one of the boys knew something. I only had to figure out which one screwed all of us. And when I figured it out, I was going to do everything in my power to destroy him.

9

Reese

T-minus four days, and here I was, a cop, a woman who'd promised to serve and protect, to uphold the law at any and all cost to myself, dropping an envelope of staged photos into a mailbox while I wore a pair of blue vinyl gloves and a hoodie, while the photo subject sat waiting for me in the car.

We'd bought a burner cell for the ransom call. And I'd spent the afternoon toughening up by watching a Sons of Anarchy marathon. Kidnapping and bad biker boys weren't exactly the same, but it put me in the criminal frame of mind. Which wasn't near as much fun as the love slave frame of mind Ryder and I had been assuming in alternate turns.

When I climbed back into the car, Ryder smiled and leaned across the console to kiss me. Soft and sweet. Sensual and sexy. If there was one thing this man could do well—

and there were several, actually—kissing would've ranked high on that list. And he had a thousand kinds of kisses. The slow, sultry promise was one of my favorites. Right next to the desperate, frenzied come-get-me mash of mouth against mouth. And the not to be forgotten until-the-morning-comes-goodnight kiss that made all my dreams about him. Those were my favorites, but to be honest, I liked them all.

He pulled the car onto the road away from his mother's brick encased mailbox then glanced over. "I had a thought."

"Yeah?"

I didn't mean to sound like I was surprised, but he wrinkled his brow and snorted. "What does that mean?"

"It means 'Yeah. What was your thought?' What's your problem?"

He didn't look at me all the way to the house. Didn't speak either and when we got back he stayed in the garage when I went inside. I didn't have much experience with male moods since I'd grown up without a man in the house, and I hadn't dated much before or after Ryder. I figured he would work his issue out and then come apologize for being a tool.

Instead, he stormed into the house and stood between me and the television with his hands on his hips. And I wouldn't have minded so much, but Bachelor in Paradise was on in reruns, and I wanted to watch.

"Hey, it's a rose ceremony. And you're blocking the screen."

"So watching reality TV is more important than talking to me." Holy crap. He was in a mood.

"They go on commercial every seven minutes. Can you hang on that long or…" I lifted my hands and gave a sarcastic head shake. Something about his moping/pouting irritated me. This was not the way I pictured a real relationship. Or maybe it was and that was why I never had one before.

"Seven minutes." He crossed his arms and tapped one foot, blowing angry bull breaths out his nose. "Seriously."

I clicked the remote and the TV went silent. "What's wrong?"

"You think I'm stupid, right? Because I didn't finish college and I tend bar and sweep floors. That I'm not good enough?" There was such hurt on his face, deepening the lines around his mouth and eyes, I just wanted to make him smile. "You're a snob."

Oh. One of us had a little complex about his jobs, and it wasn't me. "I never said any of that." I stood and sexy walked around the coffee table, continued until I was close enough to slide my hands under his shirt, feel his chest, and press my mouth against his throat. "I like that you tend bar. My dream night"—I pulled him down for a kiss—"is to have a very sexy and very naked you delivering me a margarita in bed. And then I want you to lie back and let me show you how grateful I am."

"Are you making fun of me?" But he was smiling.

I ground my hips against his. "No. I really want a margarita and I really want you to deliver it to me in bed." And afterward, when we were both basking in the afterglow, I'd ask what made him think I felt that way and what he'd been thinking in the car, but not now. Afterglow was the key.

He wrapped his arms around me and kissed the tip of my nose. "You have tequila?" I cocked an eyebrow and he chuckled. I always had tequila. "What about triple sec?"

I laughed. I was more of a two-step drink maker. Jack and coke. Rum and Kool-aid. Tequila and lime. More than that was too much work for a drink. "No, but I think I have a shaker of salt maybe an old packet of margarita mix."

But before we could go further, the burner cell rang. I looked at Ryder, at his widened eyes. "Answer it."

Yes! "Right." I picked it up and swiped the screen then turned on the speakerphone function. "Hello."

"I want you to know I have video of you putting the envelope in my mailbox and of your car driving off. I'm sending it to the police as we speak." Her voice was steel. The same one she'd used all those years ago when we'd met in her backyard and she'd told me I would have to sign a prenup if I ever married Ryder. "It's only a matter of time before they enhance it, get your license plate number and find you. And when they do…"

I clicked the end button. There went my career. My reputation. My life. Because this woman certainly didn't sound like the kind who was willing to forgive and forget. More she sounded like the kind who would vaporize her enemies if she had a special magic wand that allowed it.

"Shit." We'd driven there and away in my rental that would be traced back to me. With virtually no legwork on the part of the cops. They could figure it out, ruin me, and all it would take would be a phone call to the car company. "Fuck!"

Ryder ran his hand through his hair. "It's okay. Calm down. I'm going to handle this."

"How?"

He shrugged and my stomach rolled. "I'll call and tell her it was a joke."

"You're kidding me, right? Because the last person on earth I would expect to take a joke is your mother." Again, a picture of her vaporizing her enemies—me—flipped into my mind. "I'm going to lose my job. Lose my house and Mom's house. I'm going to jail." Oh shit. "You know what they do to cops in jail?" Watching five hours of Sons of Anarchy hadn't helped my imagination one bit.

He put a hand on each of my shoulders and gave me a little shake. "Calm down. It's going to be okay."

"You don't know." My heart was hammering and my palms were soaked. The room was starting to spin. "Shit." I swayed and Ryder caught me against his chest.

"It's okay. Breathe." He sat down and pulled me onto his lap. "It's okay. Shh."

It took a minute for my head to clear. But when it did, the visions of his mother came back. "Fuck. This is...I can't lose my job, Ryder."

"You're not going to lose your job." He smoothed my hair, then ran his hand over my spine. "Look at me." He tilted my chin up and for a second I thought he had the most beautiful eyes I'd ever seen. The most beautiful every-thing. "I let you down before, handled every single thing wrong. So I know you don't have a reason to trust me. But

I'm going to fix this. I promise. You're not going to lose your job or your house or anything else. You have my word."

His word didn't stop me from staring out the window waiting for the Maine State Police or the Glouster PD to ring my doorbell.

One Decade Ago

THE CROWD outside the Alpha house grew with every minute. Signs. Chanting. Loud shots for justice against the Alphas. There were girls crying. I wasn't close enough to the front to see who threw the first rock, but even over the crowd noise, the sound of the glass breaking echoed in my head.

Campus police pushed the crowd off the lawn then set up barriers and yelled commands the crowd ignored. Avery Stroh bumped into my shoulder, knocking me into Felicity Fields, the Chancellor's daughter. I knew them both vaguely, but hugged Avery when she pulled me out of the way of a flying beer bottle that shattered on the road next to me.

All I wanted was to see Ryder, to make sure he was okay. And maybe ask him about the girl in the video with him—Beth Cooper, a woman I knew all too well, but this was bigger than Ryder and unraveling quickly.

Felicity pulled us away from the crowd. "Come on. Let's get out of here."

I walked next to Avery. She had cut her hair off, turned

it almost as white-blonde as mine, and shed her years of black eyeliner and lipstick. She'd traded her raggedy black jeans for a pair of blue jeans and her torn crop top for a tank top covered by a blue paisley scarf. She looked unrecognizable compared to the girl I'd met freshman year.

Felicity, on the other hand, was fresh-faced with her ponytail high in the back and her jeans low in the front. She had a delicate silver chain clasped over her bare midriff and her black pumps clacked with every foot we moved away from the frat house.

When we got to the coffee shop, it was empty. Not surprising since almost everyone from the college was standing out on Fraternity Road watching the action or protesting the house.

As soon as we had our drinks, we took a table in the corner by the window. Apparently, they didn't know each other better than I knew them because Felicity held out her hand to Avery. "Felicity Fields, co-star of Finn Makenzie."

Avery replied with, "Avery Stroh, and Keaton Shaw made me a porn star." She turned to me, hand extended, one eyebrow cocked.

"I'm Reese Winthrop. I date Ryder." They looked at each other then at me.

"Date like…" Avery wiggled her eyebrows. "Or date like movie theater and hands touching over the popcorn? Or date like we're all going to Vegas for the porn awards this year?"

"I don't have a video." They looked at each other. "It doesn't prove Ryder is…the one."

"Keaton, Finn, Jameson, and Ryder are the only Alphas

they brought to the police station so far." Avery pursed her lips. "It's Keaton's boat. And Finn has the most videos. Jameson is the computer guru. And I heard Ryder made all the money."

Fuck. Was that how he paid for Boston? A weekend inside the fanciest hotel I'd ever been to. Room service. Champagne and chocolate-covered strawberries. Then the trip to Camden where we spent a few days hiking and relaxing at the cutest bed and breakfast. Oh, God. The necklace.

I ran a finger over the teardrop diamond. Shit.

"Who did you hear that from?"

Again, they looked at each other. "Finn." Felicity closed her eyes.

Avery shook her head and took a long drink of her iced coffee. "I don't know about the two of you, but I'm not feeling all stand-by-my-man. I'm more thinking I'm in the he-better-hope-I-don't-ever-get-access-to-a-gun situation."

Felicity's pensive, curious look could easily have been mistaken for constipation. "You're Ryder's girl." She looked at Avery. Something silent passed between them again. "I don't want to freak you out or anything, but...Finn said Ryder was all twisted over Avery and Keaton being together."

What? "I don't know what you mean."

She opened her mouth and Avery put a hand on her arm. "She's...It's nothing. It's Finn's imagination gone wild. Don't listen to her." She turned to Felicity. "And shame on you for repeating weird gossip. Right now, we need to figure out what to do. How to help them. Or if we should." She adjusted her scarf, then adjusted it some more, and finally unwound it and flung it on the floor. "Holy shit. All of you straight-laced bitches wear a lot of unnecessary clothes." She sighed, looked at me, and pursed her lips. "Finn has it wrong. It wasn't…I was the one with the crush. I asked Keaton to help me…be what Ryder wanted. You know. A Sigma. Soft-spoken. Gentler. But I ended up… happily, I mean…until now…with Keaton." She paused and I wished I'd stayed at the frat house. No way could I compete with Avery Stroh. "And you have Ryder."

But did I? Did I really? And knowing everything I knew, did I even want him? Felicity pulled a laptop from her shoulder bag. "I want to check and see if the website is still up." She clicked the keys, closed her eyes, and hit enter. A second later, she typed some more. "Website's down, but some Einstein reposted all the videos."

"You're probably going to have to go to the police to get them removed permanently."

Avery shook her head. "I went today before they arrested…or whatever…" Her sigh sounded so sad. "Anyway, the cops said they can't really prove who posted the videos so unless someone confesses…" She looked over my shoulder. "Holy shit! Look at that."

The TV hanging in the corner was tuned to the news and the on-scene—at the marina—reporter stood in front of the boat where Ryder and I had spent so many nights. "Oh my God."

"Was it the protestors?"

"Maybe one of the Alpha brothers is trying to protect

Ryder and Finn and Keaton and Jameson." It was reasonable. Even if my statement lacked the conviction I'd intended.

"Or maybe the guys are trying to hide evidence." We were probably all thinking it. I was just glad Avery was the one who said it.

The newscast ended with footage of the guys leaving the police station individually. Felicity stared at the table and traced a heart carved into the wood. "I know I should want to go to find them, but…" She puffed one cheek and blew the breath out slow. "I don't want him to lie to me about it."

"Maybe he won't." Of course he would. If he was smart, he would find a good story and stick to it. No matter who he was talking to. Especially if it was one of the girls who'd ended up in an online video with him and he'd been arrested for it.

Avery finally glanced away from the TV. "Then he's stupid. If he doesn't figure out a good spin, all of them, they're going to jail. This could even be federal since it was online."

Every facet of this felt off. Wrong. And until I talked to Ryder, heard him admit what he'd done, I was going to stand by him. But if he did this…all bets were off.

10

Ryder

I didn't have any choice. I had to go see her. My mother. The woman who cut me off from the family fortune, forced me into homelessness, and refused to release even a dollar of my trust fund even though it was mine and I needed it. I wasn't any more bitter. But I wasn't any less bitter either.

She "received" me on the back patio, but insisted I walk around the outside of the house, as if she didn't even want me inside her precious showplace. The table was covered in plastic and the chairs had been taken away so I had nothing to do but stand and wait for her to make her appearance. And wait I did. Ten minutes. Then twenty. An hour. And she damned well knew what she was doing.

Finally, she stepped outside, head to toe Prada, martini in one hand, ransom pictures in the other. "I could have you arrested."

I nodded. I didn't want to start off arguing and "could have" was very much different than the "going to have" I expected. "I know. I'm sorry."

She scoffed. "You've always been such a disappointment."

That hurt. "When I was top of my class every year since kindergarten? Or when I was a state all-star in football, baseball, and hockey?"

She scoffed and finished her drink in one long gulp. "Since you came out of my womb looking like your no good lazy father." Not something I could control, but I wasn't here to fight. "What do you want, Ryder?"

Dear God, this sucked. "To apologize. To ask for those pictures back."

She wrinkled her nose. "I appreciate the sentiment behind the apology, but I think, knowing you as I do, the sincerity will be lacking. And you know how I feel about sincerity." She continued and because there was nothing more she liked than hearing herself go on, and on, and on, I remained silent. "And honesty. That's where we've always been on opposite sides, you and I."

"I never thought we were on opposite sides, Mom." She was the only one who'd ever been allowed to have a side.

Another scoff, this one more sarcastic than the last. "You chose early. I can't blame you, I suppose. Your father always presented himself to you in a better light than I could. I had to make the money and do the work. He got to listen to you read, watch you play ball, eat dinners with you. I had to be the disciplinarian."

I would've loved to do those things with her when I was

growing up. But she'd acted like my bank more than my mother. My judgmental, restrictive bank. She controlled—or tried to control—me with money.

My heart pinged. "It's not too late."

She cocked an eyebrow as if she was considering it. Then she stomped. On me. Not with her actual shoes, but I couldn't imagine that hurting more. "I couldn't possibly risk being seen with you now. You've disgraced yourself and your father and our family. To bring you back into the fold would…it's impossible."

I nodded because I couldn't speak. Could barely breathe. I turned to walk away, to never see my mother again, to get the fuck out of there before I started bawling like some pathetic child. I made it almost to the edge of the patio when she cleared her throat. "Ryder." I turned. Pathetically hopeful she'd changed her mind. Wanted a hug. "Here." She held the photos out. "This way you don't have to come back."

I took the pictures and walked—half-jogged back to Reese's rental car. I closed myself inside and collapsed, chest heaving, not enough air in the world for my lungs. The tears came, and I didn't bother trying to stop them, even as I started the car and drove. Aimless.

I found myself in front of the Alpha house. It hadn't changed much. The trees were still trimmed, the lawn still edged. The porch still adorned with redwood Adirondak chairs with a cooler between them and the Alpha banner hanging from the eaves at the highest point of the front façade. Lights shone in each window. But for all its similarities to ten years ago, so much was different. So many changes.

I drove on. Past the sorority houses—Gammas and Sigmas and Deltas—to make a left. There was Chancellor Fields' place, the chaplain's house. I stopped at the edge of the driveway.

So many memories.

"Here. Let me help you with that." The biker princess stepped back from the box, and I carried it up the stairs to the room over the garage. I set it on a table. She hadn't been struggling, but I was mowing the chaplain's grass when she pulled up on her bike and she was hot. Really hot. So doable with her coal black hair, eyes lined dark, mouth full and kissable. Fuck. My dick stood at attention begging for an introduction. "I'm Ryder."

"Avery."

God, I'd wanted her so bad. And Keaton got her. I hated him for it, but then I met Reese and everything worked out. For a while. Until I got stupid and greedy.

From the Chaplain's house, I drove to the bar. And drank. I didn't speak to anyone other than the bartender and only then to order another shot, another beer.

And like some damned fool, a true and honest to God idiot, I walked, because I had misplaced Reese's keys, to Avery's.

They were all there. Keaton, Finn, Jameson...a decade of regrets. "Did you know..." The story poured out in broken bits. I'd wanted Avery. The memory was clouded and dusty, but I hated Keaton. Then for getting Avery. Now for being happy when I just kept losing at life. Me. Ryder Fucking Kennedy. Stumbling drunk and losing at life.

After he made me watch him kiss the girl—big surprise —he nodded at Finn. "You wanna take care of this."

Finn looked at me. "Fuck him. He can find his own way home."

Drunk or not. I couldn't blame him. Felicity tilted her head. "Come on, Finn." She held me up under one arm and he took the other side. "Did you drink *all* the beer in town?" She grumbled as she and Finn walked me out the door to a small SUV and propped me against the side as she opened the door and Finn held me up by my chest.

"Drinking problem?" Even hammered, I could hear the snide in his tone.

"Thinking problem." The correction didn't mean much. Less because he ignored it and shoved me into the seat.

"Do not puke in my car." Luck wasn't on his side. Or mine.

From the passenger seat, Felicity turned and leaned around to look at me. "You want to go back to Reese's place?"

Finn answered before I could. "You think it's smart since he just confessed his undying love for Avery?"

"Oh, my God, Finn. He didn't confess undying love. He confessed to a crush." That was right. *You tell him, Felicity.*

"He said he lost the girl of his dreams."

God love Felicity. She knew me. Heard me. "He didn't say Avery was the girl of his dreams. He just said he lost her. He meant Reese."

Hell yeah, I did. "Yeah! You don't know everything, Finn."

"Shut up, back there. Before I forget you're a drunk and I give you the ass-kicking you deserve."

"Ah, the payback beating." I didn't remember everything that happened that day, but I remembered enough. Back then, Finn was a running back who'd never learned to take a hit because I protected his ass. I blocked. I kept him safe so he could rush for the most yards in a single season record. "Take your shot."

"Don't tempt me."

"Jesus, you guys. We're grown-ups now." Felicity huffed and puffed as Finn and I continued to taunt each other.

"I just want to know one thing." Finn shifted to glance at me in the rearview. "Why did you kick my ass?"

"You uploaded the videos." Like he didn't know. Like it didn't make sense.

He shook his head. "No, I didn't."

I gripped both front seats by their inner edges and pulled myself forward. Needed to see his face when he lied. So later, when I could stand straight, I could make sense of it. "Yes, you did." Ha. Ha. I needed to argue so he would lie to me again.

He half twisted to look at me then turned back to the road then swiveled his head again. "No, I fucking didn't." He shook his head and slammed the butt of his palm against the steering wheel. "I let your dad into your fucking room to drop off cash, you little trust fund bitch. I never went in there." He shook his head. "I knew you thought that. But it wasn't me."

"Well, it wasn't me. Keaton was at practice, Jameson was getting a scan of his knee." I could remember that day so clearly. I was with Reese at a fall carnival. We'd gotten our pictures taken—sans timestamp that could've saved my ass—on hay bales with piping hot cider and a man dressed as a scarecrow dressed as Santa. "You were homesick. Remember?"

"Look, I let your dad into your room. Then Beth Cooper came by. I went for a steam. You know to sweat out whatever I had going on. Came back, your dad was leaving."

Beth Cooper. Dad. Well, now all the holes had a cover. Or whatever the saying said that meant I understood.

He pulled the car over. Swerved like the steering went out and he was fighting for control, when in actuality, he was likely just being pissy. When he turned to face me, the car rolled forward because he had stopped, but not put the car in park. He corrected then glared at me. "You kicked my ass for nothing."

It wasn't for nothing. But I couldn't tell him that without letting a very dangerous cat out of a very thin bag. "Sorry about that." Drunk me could be gracious. Apologetic even. But drunk or sober, no way could I be honest. Not until I had all the proof. Facts.

"Sorry?" He scoffed and shook his head. "He's sorry."

"Did you want me to kiss it better?" The old Finn would've laughed, shoved me, maybe even slammed on the brakes to pitch me forward. I held my breath, waiting to see how much of my old friend was left in there.

It took a second, but he laughed. "You're an idiot."

Not a headline. "So I hear." And didn't I know it? I had too many important things going on without having to deal with a hangover. Too many things to do to fix this shit show without having to stop every ten minutes for Gatorade and Advil.

"If it wasn't me and it wasn't you, and it wasn't Jameson or Keaton, then who?" He was skeptical. I didn't blame him. We'd reached the I-know-but-can't-tell portion of our evening and I went into defensive mode.

"I'm still not sure it wasn't you."

He shot me a glare in the rear-view. "I'm a doctor now and I don't do a lot of fist fighting, but I'm pretty sure I can take your drunk ass, so I'd think very hard about what you say next." I nodded at him. Nothing he said would surprise me now. "What if it was Beth? She went up to your room. Maybe she knew about the video you made of you guys together."

Possible, but less likely and only half as true as what I believed—but couldn't speak about—actually happened. "Did anybody besides Beth and my dad show up?"

He cocked an eyebrow I could see in the mirror. "Not before I went to steam. I don't know about after."

The alcohol and all the information in my brain went to war. I couldn't sort it properly enough to make a conclusion. I couldn't even see in single vision with both eyes open. I squeezed the left one shut and wished it was so easy to make my brain work right.

There had to be a way to figure it out, but until I slept off the effects of spending an afternoon drinking after so many afternoons of abstinence, no way was I going to be able to do more than throw up on the back of Finn's seat. Which I did. Then passed out.

. . .

One Decade Ago

So, today was the day all my dreams of becoming a lawyer, of joining the family law firm—Kennedy, Kennedy, and Grimes, my parents held the first two-thirds of the partnership—circled the sewer drain. The day I lost my last best friend. The day the girl I loved left me. Nothing I could do to stop it.

Especially not hungover. Which I was. Hungover. And stupid. Stupid as fuck for trusting Finn. For believing he would've ever stuck by me, been my friend. They were all against me now. And it was him. He was the bastard that uploaded the videos. Had to be. No one else was in the frat house. Only Finn.

And today, since he couldn't have acted without me—no videos, no upload—I was going, and even I couldn't believe how strongly I felt about it, to admit not only my part but take credit or blame, as it were, for his. It would be one noble act in a long life of ignoble.

I was focused. Determined. Ready to take whatever happened so I could earn the redemption I needed.

That was what I told myself. More it was so the extent of what I'd done didn't cast light on anyone else. I couldn't take the chance Finn figured out what actually happened. The destruction would be total. Life-shattering.

And as noble as I wanted to be, I hated being in this position. My guts ached. My head throbbed. Truth was, having to do this pissed me off.

Anger simmered in that little area of dead space just under the skin, tingled through every nerve I had, and put a shitty taste in my mouth.

I left my car a couple blocks away because the street was closed off. The protests had taken over. And none of them supported me. Why would they? My side wasn't out there. I couldn't even tell my side.

I circled along the back of Chancellor Hall. "Hey."

Oh, God. Of all the people I could face, Reese Winthrop wasn't one I wanted to. Not now when I had to stay focused and be strong enough to do the right thing.

She laid her hand on my arm, and I stopped walking. I wanted to kiss her. To thank her for coming because it made me feel better. Made me want to tell everything so she didn't think any worse of me. But those were dangerous thoughts. Dangerous for me and for her. Because I couldn't let her think good things about me. She would try to change everyone's mind, try to make me look better, feel better, try to prove it wasn't me. I couldn't afford that.

"What?" My tone was hard, brutal.

"I tried to call you." Our dynamic already changed. Her voice thinned, weakened. She was ready for me to hurt her. Bracing herself for it.

And that made me a jackass. "What do you want, Reese?"

Her eyes went wide, like she couldn't believe I was acting this way. But if that was honestly the case, then she didn't know me at all. This was who I was. Who I was born to be. "I just wanted to be here with you. For you."

Every word tore me down a little more. Removed another option. "I don't want you here."

Hurt flickered in her eyes, but she lifted her chin. "Ryder, are you pissed off at me?"

Oh, God. I steeled myself against the urge to comfort her. Being with me, from this day forward, would destroy her. I'd taken enough from her.

"What do you want from me, Reese? I'm trying to break it to you gently. Do you want me to just say it?" Oh fuck. I just had to get through this. So I could get to the next shitty part of my day. She didn't speak. "Did you really think you were someone I could be with?" I shook my head and swallowed a mouthful of bile. "For the love of God, Reese. I've dated Sigmas and Deltas. Did you honestly think you could compete? That you were more than a very grateful fuck?" Her eyes clouded and her lower lip quivered. "You're too plain. Too ordinary. Hell, if you didn't give such a fabulous blow job, I wouldn't have wasted near the time I did."

"Ryder."

My guts twisted. "So, unless you wanna get on your knees right now, I don't think we really have anything else to talk about." I nodded toward the building ahead on my left. "I have a meeting to get to so I need you to get the hell out of my way."

She stayed long enough for me to see the tears in her eyes, for me to know what I'd done, then she turned, and ran. And I couldn't blame her.

Worst moment of my life. Hands down.

I walked a few feet before it occurred to me I couldn't chase her. I couldn't do what I had to do with her by my side. I wouldn't because she would push me to do the right thing. Not this.

It was better for her to hate me. Probably better for me to hate myself.

"Dude, that was brutal."

"Shut the fuck up, Finn." I knew what it was. "What are you doing here? You aren't scheduled to testify until later."

"I'm going in now. I'm going to tell them…" I couldn't let him finish. The only way this worked was if I accepted all the blame. Not had it thrown at me. And I couldn't take the chance with Finn. He'd stopped talking to me, thanks to our fucking lawyers who said we couldn't afford to be seen together. And my lawyer had told me I needed to find a way to blame the others or pick one to blame, so I had to assume his was giving him the same advice.

But the only way my friends walked away free was if I made sure this shit didn't touch them. I swung, hard. And when my fist hit his jaw…a bit of anguish drained from my gut. But it all came swinging back when he didn't hit back. A final blow took him down and this time, he didn't get back up, didn't even move. I checked to make sure he was okay and breathing.

When I was finished, I stood, wiped my bloodied hand on his shirt then adjusted my clothes. Just because I'd been in a fight—one-sided or not—didn't mean I could afford to walk in there looking like it.

And goddamn, Finn, anyway. He was going to go in and sell me out. I knew it. Not because he was the kind of guy to turn on a friend, but because he was honest. No matter what. Brutally honest. And if I was going down, fuck him. He could come along for the ride.

And I held that thought, toyed with it, until I walked in and saw all the people waiting to hear what the Glouster Four had to say. Then, I knew. Finn was the best friend I ever had. The only true friend. A guy who'd stuck by me. Probably would've continued to had I not made him my punching bag.

I walked in and stared at the Chancellors. Chancellor Fields called the meeting to order then sat back in his chair. "Mr. Kennedy, do you have an opening statement?"

I nodded. "Yes, sir." Then with one small breath, I threw my future and everything I ever hoped to be out the window.

11

Reese

There were a hundred things I would've rather done than tuck a drunken guy into the bed I slept in, but he was too tall for the sofa and the guest room had about six thousand boxes stacked on top of it.

I pulled his shoes off and set them by the door, then tried—valiantly tried—to remove his jacket, but he wrapped his arms around my waist and flipped me onto the bed next to him. "What are you doing?"

"Holding the girl of my dreams." He tucked me against his chest and let his chin rest on the top of my head. He sighed, contented, happy by the sound of it. "Did you change your hair and clothes because of me? Because I was a dick to you?"

Yes. That was one-hundred percent of the reason. "No." I couldn't think of a lie fast enough. It had, over the years, made undercover work easier. But that had nothing to do with the initial change.

"Did I hurt you?"

Hurt? No. He'd destroyed me. "I'm pretty tough."

"I couldn't stop seeing your face when I closed my eyes." His thumb stroked the small of my back, and my breath hitched. Something about his touch made me want to shove my tongue in his mouth, grind my hips against his until he stripped us both, and let me screw him until he was cross-eyed and muttering incoherently. "Those things I said to you…that you were just a fuck"—I could've done without the play by play I remembered by heart—"and that I wouldn't have wasted my time on you if you didn't give such good head, I didn't mean them."

"It's okay."

He shook his head and sniffled, then again and I pulled back to look at him. He had tears. "I hurt you. Nothing about that is okay."

I wasn't strong enough to resist his regret. Hell, I wasn't even sure if I wanted to resist. Years I'd waited for his apology. Years I'd wanted to know why he'd said all those things, but right now, with his arms around me and that damned thumb still stroking, it didn't matter.

"Ryder…" If I sounded like I couldn't catch my breath, it was because I couldn't. There was too much Ryder in this room intoxicating me, making me wonder exactly how important breath really was.

"I was such a fucking fool." He sniffled again. "We could have five or six kids by now."

I chuckled. "That's pretty big numbers for the guy who doesn't have to shoot them out of his body." But I could see our kids—beautiful like Ryder, tough, but kind. But not five. Definitely not six. Two was a good number. Three maybe.

"Doesn't matter now because I'm a fucking idiot."

He spoke with such conviction, and I was in a spot in my head where those imaginary kids played that I didn't argue. I kissed his collarbone, the only place I could reach. I wanted kids. Not as much back then. They'd been more abstract, a someday, but still with Ryder. Lately though, the tick tick tick of my biological clock woke me up, and reminded me I was alone. Lonely. Five or six kids didn't sound so many now.

I was tired. Not tired as in I didn't get enough sleep. Tired as in worn out. Tired of being alone and lonely. Apparently, it made me honest. "I used to wish I would've gotten pregnant back then. I was so pathetic. I thought if I had your kid, you'd have to come back to me."

He groaned. "I would've." Groaned again when I slid my body against his so I could reach his earlobe for a nibble and a suck then threw my leg over his hip and used my calf muscle to pull him in. "Reese."

When I ground against him, he tightened his arms and closed his eyes. Then he was gone. Out of the bed. In the bathroom, gargling mouthwash, standing in the shower.

Naked when I walked in. "My dick doesn't work when I'm drunk." He hadn't bothered to close the shower curtain, and I could see every delicious inch of him. "I'm trying to sober up."

"Is this one of those hold my beer situations? Like you

tell me it doesn't work, and I'm supposed to say, 'challenge accepted'?" Because there was a really good and quite soapy chance I could've been talked into that kind of thing pretty easily.

"No, it's an I'm an idiot who drank too much situation." He bowed his head against the tiled wall next to his hands and water ran over his back, defining every muscle, making me forget everything I should've been thinking about more than how much I wanted him, but about how angry I should've been that he was drunk and here and…here.

I was strong enough not to say "hold my beer" or "challenge accepted" but only because I bit my lip. But he was naked and slick with water sluicing down his body in all the best ways. And that was a lot of glistening wet man to resist.

"Fuck." Nothing like a little desperation to rob me of the last vestiges of my dignity. I stripped off my clothes like I was trying to set a world speed record then climbed in between him and the spray of water. It soaked my hair and ran into my eyes, but I would've drowned for this minute. To have him push me against the wall, lift me by the backs of my thighs, smash his mouth against mine and devour me.

And to the contrary. Drinking did not render his cock useless. He got hard in my hand. Stayed hard in my mouth. Then again in my pussy. Hard and hot. Exciting. Amazing.

He held me with a hand on each of my hips, my ass pressed against his groin. He bucked his hips, went deeper with each thrust until I was out of control, whimpering and moaning in reply to his groans and grunts. Clawing red marks into the back of one of his thighs. I wanted him. Needed him to quench the ache inside me.

When I came, my body went rigid and I straightened, my hand seeking out the curve of his ass, muscles tight and tense. A second later, he groaned and strained, his arms strong and unyielding. His eyes squeezed shut and his lower lip pulled between his teeth. Adorable.

No wonder I was too weak to deny myself. "I guess it was a hold my beer situation." I smiled as he moved away to run his head under the spray of ever-cooling water. Once we washed each other which took a lot longer than it should've because we paid close attention to some very vital areas, he shut off the water and wrapped me in a towel.

But stopped on about the third or fourth swipe of the towel against my back. "Did you do it on purpose?" His voice was steel. Icy. Like his mother's.

"What?" He reached to the shelf behind the toilet for a towel and wrapped it around his waist then stalked out of the bathroom back to the bedroom like I'd forced myself on him.

"Hey!" I called after him, and there was no way he didn't hear me, but he kept going. By the time I convinced myself to move and arrived in the doorway, he already had his pants on and was sliding a t-shirt over his head. "Ryder?"

"You took advantage of me." His voice was a thousand nails down the chalkboard.

"I did what?" And I almost laughed at the absurdity of

it. I didn't hear him say no or ask me not to put his cock in my mouth. Kind of negated his assertion. But I still couldn't wait to hear the justification. "How did I take advantage of you?"

"Fuck me without a condom because your ovaries are crying out for a kid?" He wagged a finger in my ovary area. "Because your tits need the"—he gestured to my boobs in a knob-twisting kind of motion—"gentle suckling of a little baby to make you feel like you've checked all of life's boxes."

Every word he said was stupider than the one before it. It wasn't hard to understand how he managed to look like that and still remain single. "We had sex without a condom because you're the one who pulled me up off my knees and bent me over so you could put your dick in." There would be no blaming me. Well, a little because I'd followed him to the bathroom. But, at the risk of sounding like a broken record, I was a cop and not so desperate for a kid that my devious little mind went straight to unprotected sex makes baby for me. Surely, he had to know that. But obviously, he didn't. And that pissed me off. "You know what, Ryder? You *are* a fucking idiot."

He shook his head. "Yeah. Get what you want then call me names, right? I'm an asshole and a dick and a fucking idiot."

I scoffed when he paused. "Why don't you hold your breath while you wait for me to argue. Solve both our problems." I snatched my mom's robe off the back of the door and shoved my arms inside because I argued better when I wasn't standing mostly naked in front of the person I was having it out with.

"And let you raise my kid by yourself?" The indignance was overkill.

I rolled my eyes. "I'm going to forgive you because alcohol kills brain cells and judging by the bullshit you're spewing, I'm going to say you drank a lot. And so the couple of cells you have left aren't functioning properly—definitely not from overuse, but… Whatever. Not my place to judge. But don't say something you're going to regret later. I'm not going to let you take it back." Not a threat. He might've had the size advantage, but I had years of pent-up rage. Ryder rage.

"What does that mean?" He stuffed his shirt into his waistband a couple extra times even after it was securely tucked. Angry, fine. So was I.

But purposefully obtuse was too much. I narrowed my eyes, but he still looked like sex on a stick and my anger wavered. Later on, I would happily dissect what it said about me that I was so angry I wanted to throttle him and so hot for him I wanted to throw him down on the bed at the same time. Right now, I wanted to hit him with arrows pointed by my words.

"It means before you say something shitty that makes me hate you worse than I do now, you might want to think about it because you aren't the kind of guy who can afford to lose another friend." His eyes flickered like I'd hit the bullseye with that one.

I waited for the sting of whatever he replied. "You were never my friend. You were just the girl I was fucking."

And there it was.

One Decade Ago

"Oh, honey, are you sure?" She looked at me through the mirror in front of me. "That's a lot of stress on your hair. The extensions and the color." She had the nasal drone and big poof of shiny black hair reminiscent of eighties sitcom TV.

But I hadn't traveled to New York with all the money I'd saved over the years and decided to spend on this makeover because I wanted to pay extra for someone to second guess me. "I'm sure. Let's just do it." If my hair was too stressed, I'd shave it. Or find it a shrink. Didn't matter. I needed a drastic change and I scoured magazines and websites for days. Then I found this.

No one was ever going to mistake me for some plain Jane pushover who let people say whatever they wanted. No fucking way.

And an hour later, I checked her work in the mirror. Gone was the mousy brown, replaced by a vibrant almost silver that extended way past my shoulders thanks to the extra hair she'd woven in with mine. She explained care, took my three hundred fifty dollars plus hundred dollar tip —birthday money saved since second grade—and I picked up my bags from Vannie's Vintage and Goth Thrift which included skirts so short my ass cheeks showed, shirts ripped and tight, shoes with thick platforms and square heels. My nun days were over.

I drove straight back, pulled into Felicity's driveway, and smiled when she stumbled over a "Can I help you?" before she recognized me.

"Holy shit. What did you do?"

"Let's see that bastard call me plain now." I pushed past her into the living room of her place and sighed. She knew what had happened between Ryder and me, and she understood.

"They—the Alphas—had court today. An arraignment."

I didn't want to ask, but… "Did everything…come out… okay…for Finn?" We both knew who I was asking about.

She pursed her lips. "They dropped the charges against all of them." Her eyes lowered and her voice came softer. "Except Ryder." And much brighter, she added, "But it looks like he's going to take a deal."

I nodded, trying not to think of him in jail or worse. Closing my eyes as of my imagination would be stopped by a couple of eyelids. "What kind of deal?"

"I don't know all the details. I think restitution. Maybe a couple months in jail." I think. Maybe. These were not the absolutes I needed. I couldn't stand the thought of him in jail. For whatever reason, the idea of Ryder behind bars with hardened criminals made my stomach turn. My throat was clogged with tears or anger or something almost too big to breathe around, anyway. Two breaths stood between me and a quick meltdown. And once I took those, there was nothing holding me together. I cried. And I wanted to roll up into a ball and pretend I hadn't made a fool of myself, but then she wrapped me in a hug.

"They all suck, Reese." She patted my back and stroked

my hair and shushed me until I was finally cried out. Then she helped me wash off and reapply the mascara that had streaked down my face. She wouldn't meet my eyes though. Not until she said, "You want to hear something… crazy?" I nodded because friends shared crazy stories. At least they did on TV. So yeah. We did, too. "I married Finn."

My fingers curled into fists at my side. I needed to change the subject. "So, married, huh?"

Her skin flushed. "He's amazing." She filled in some generic details. Called him wonderful, sweet, more than she imagined. But swore she didn't love him.

I stared at her. Checked for any sign she was kidding. She wasn't. "Oh shit." I needed details. "When?"

"It's been eleven days today." She sniffed and her voice crept to one of those ear-shattering heights. "My eleventh anniversary." I'd never seen an honest to God panic attack before, but if that wasn't what I was witnessing then I didn't know what it was. She shook her hands out hard until her knuckles cracked, and she hopped. On one foot. In a circle. Her breaths were short and shallow. Like Lamaze breaths. "I married Finn Makenzie." I nodded because I didn't know what sound was going to make her worse. "And he's getting kicked out of school. For good."

Oh shit. That meant they all were. "It's going to be okay."

"No. I don't know if I can be with someone who…got kicked out of the school my dad runs." But that wasn't what she meant. She meant someone who was kicked out of school. I half wondered if that made her a snob, but I got dumped by a guy who got kicked out of school so I couldn't judge.

I took her by the shoulders. "Do you love him?"

"He deserves someone who is sure..." At least she wasn't dancing around anymore.

"You're allowed to doubt." God knew I did. I didn't just doubt. I hated. Vowed to hate Ryder for as long as I lived.

The tears in her eyes spilled over. "He wouldn't doubt me." He wouldn't. Finn believed in everyone. It was kind of his thing. Kindness. Faith in people. And to die for looks.

But I wasn't afflicted with such belief in people. And it didn't take a genius to know he'd married her to legitimize himself. "Felicity..." I had to make her see he was only protecting himself. Was using her. Was not the person she thought. None of them were.

She held up her hand. "Please, don't. I love Finn, and I know it seems like we only did this to...and it started that way. But I've never been so happy. I wake up every morning looking into that guy's face." She shook her head. "Even if it ends right now, I wouldn't regret it."

There was some courage in that statement. A definable determination. It gave me hope for them. She loved him. That would get them through. "It won't end, Fliss. I can see you guys in fifty years sitting on a porch in front of a house with those little garden gnomes and flower boxes under the windows. You guys'll make it."

She grinned. Who didn't like hearing how happy they were going to be for the rest of their lives. "You think so?"

"Of course, I do." I hugged her. "I have news, too, kind

of." She cocked her head. "I'm going to enroll in the police academy in San Jose."

"California?" Her voice did that pitchy high octave thing again.

I nodded. It was as far away from Ryder Kennedy and a university full of bad memories as I could get. "It isn't going to work out for me here."

Oh no. She frowned and her chin quivered. "But we just got to know each other."

I would miss her and Avery. This video scandal brought us together. Maybe it wasn't all bad. Well, worse for them than for me since Ryder hadn't uploaded anything with us together so my naked ass wasn't stored in anyone's cloud. But they'd acted like we were all in it together even when some of the other victims called them traitors for sticking by Keaton and Finn.

"We can talk on the phone and write letters. And we can visit." Even to me, the words sounded empty, like something people said, but never did. "We just have to make sure we make it a priority."

"It's all the way across the country." She widened her eyes and puffed out her cheeks. The distance was my favorite part.

We both needed a hug. Fortunately, she knew how to make such a thing happen without also making it awkward. "I've never had friends like you and Avery. I'm not going to give you guys up. We'll figure it out."

She smiled. "You bet."

And if it hadn't fallen apart for us by then, it was coming. Faster than we could protect ourselves.

12

Ryder

Hungover. And worse, I had full memory of every stupid word I said and every stupid thing I did. How I hurt Reese again. Fuck.

Just the girl I was fucking. I'd said some dumbass things before, but that had to be top of the list. She hadn't kicked me out. Hadn't asked me to leave. Hadn't even spoken another word, just went into her mother's room, closed the door, and shut me out. Not that I could blame her. I didn't want to see me right then either.

But now it was morning. And I scrolled down my to-do list. Fix this. That was definitely at the top. Then find a way for Reese to keep the house. Finally, make sure my mom knew I was happy. Washing dishes and mopping floors might not have been the most glamorous job, but it was honest work.

But my mom wasn't here and lottery numbers weren't being drawn until Saturday, so since I was here… I knocked on the bedroom door. "Reese?" I waited a good two minutes then lifted my hand to knock again as the door opened.

"I thought you were leaving."

I pointed to the pants on the floor in the attached bathroom. "You locked yourself in with my pants."

She turned, walked calmly to the bathroom, snatched the jeans off the floor, and brought them back to hold out between us. When I didn't take them, she shook them twice and the envelope of photos she'd sent Mom fell on the floor. She threw the pants over her shoulder then picked up the pictures.

"You went to see your mom." She chuckled then shook her head. "Captain Obvious couldn't have been more… obvious." I knew the exact moment she figured it out. Her eyes went wide and she swiped her tongue along the right corner of her lips. "That's why you…came here drunk."

I shrugged and she waved the envelope then slapped it against her forehead twice. "You could've only gotten them from her." I knew what she was thinking. All the same things I thought about my mother. Their first meeting, and every subsequent one since then, had been ugly. Thanks to Mom.

"She turned her back on you. Cut you out of her life. And for me, you went there?" Her eyes pooled with tears and one slipped down each cheek before she used the inside of her wrist on one cheek and the outside on the other to smear them away. "In light of this new information, I am definitely the asshole."

I grinned. "Why don't you hold your breath while you wait for me to argue." Her words.

"That sounds fair, I guess."

"Familiar, at least." The anguish on her face made me want to hold her, but I remained leaning against the doorframe while she sat on the bed. I didn't trust myself to move further into the room. But when she started to cry, I couldn't stand there and not do something.

"Reese…" Hugging her made sense. Tilting her chin up to kiss the tears away, also reasonable. Lying back and holding her wasn't even optional but required.

She laid her head on my chest and put her hand on my heart. "Every time I think I have you figured out, you go and do something…" Her fingers grasped a handful of my shirt. "There are always going to be those people who think you deserved worse than you got, and to some people, you're always going to be the guy who videoed a bunch of unsuspecting women then made money off it. But to me, you're always going to be the guy who went into the dragon's lair to save me from…"

"The dragon lady." I finished her thought because she wouldn't. In all the time she'd known of the situation and how my mom behaved, she'd never said a bad word about her.

"Something like that." But she hugged me tighter, curled into my side, and stroked her finger across the space above my heart.

I didn't want all these minutes between us to be heavy, burdensome, and sad. "So, I guess what you're saying is… I'm your hero." This was the guy I wanted to be. The one she made me into. She gave me back all the pieces of myself I shit on when I installed those cameras.

"My very own knight in shining Levis." She turned to rest her hands under her chin across my chest. I could see every fleck of blue in her eyes, every flutter of her lashes, every tiny freckle on her skin. Nothing in the world made me feel so protective, so enamored. "I've always wanted to say something to you."

"Okay." As long as she wasn't telling me to get out again, she could say whatever she wanted.

She blew out a breath. "The day that we stopped talking to each other…" God, I wished I could erase that day from her memory. And mine. It shamed me, hurt that I'd lost her over my own stupidity. But I didn't want to interrupt. "That day…it was…I knew you were having one of the worst days of your life, and I might not have been honest with, well, with myself. Or you. I blamed you, but like I said, I knew how awful things were." She closed her eyes. "I didn't call because…I didn't know how I felt…about what you did."

Not that I hadn't expected it, but her words hurt, caused a physical ache in my chest. But not more than I deserved. "It's okay."

"It's not okay." She shook her head. "Brace yourself, because some serious self-enlightenment is on the way." She smiled, but it looked almost sad. "I am not someone who should be allowed to judge the goodness of others." She scoffed and tilted her head. "But I did that to you. Over and over. Hell, I did it last night."

I deserved whatever she thought about me. Not only was I the reason there was a Glouster Four, I used it to hurt her. I was the hit that kept on hitting when it came to her. A better man would walk away again, but I wasn't one of those.

"Reese, everybody has stuff…things to overcome." I cradled her closer for a second. "Please, don't make me recite my list. I don't think we have that kind of lifetime." Easy to joke when the joke was so close to the truth but not quite.

"I don't need the list to know you." She slid her body up so we were nose to nose and she could stroke my cheek. "You're my dragon slayer."

Oh, God. I was falling for her. Again. And I needed to apologize. Again. "I'm sorry for what I said last night. There was never a time for me when you were just the girl I was fucking."

She closed her eyes. "I know."

There were about a thousand things about her I didn't deserve. Her compassion was a huge one. I wasn't worthy. "You know?" Of course she knew, but… "Reese, I don't want to be the guy who says things he shouldn't and then has to apologize later. And it seems like that's all I ever end up doing. Apologizing to you."

She breathed in and buried her head in my shoulder. "You don't always have to apologize." But I did. "We'll be better. Both of us."

For once, I had hope. I had the idea of a tomorrow worth waking up for. One where a genuine smile didn't seem abstract and so far away. "I promise."

She pulled back and smiled. "And even if we're not together"—cue record scratch.

"What?"

"I-I'm just saying, if the path leads us...shit. I live in California. And I'm losing the house...I've left here before and promised to come back to visit. It took my mom dying to get me on a plane." She was killing me. Taking away my hope.

"What the hell does that mean?" I was going to need it in plain English. No more pussy-footing through a field of nice words.

"I'm saying, I don't think...I don't think we should plan a big bright future that isn't going to happen. I'm here for a little while. Let's enjoy that."

Enjoy that? "What?" *Not going to happen* pretty much didn't leave room for misinterpretation.

"Well, tell me, Ryder. Are you moving to California?" Sun. Sand. Beaches. Winter warmth. Sounded good to me. But I didn't answer out of sheer pigheaded obstinance. "Because I'm not really a video chat kind of girl."

Dear God, I couldn't lose her again. Fuck!

"I thought you wanted to try to keep the house." I was grasping at straws. Any one I could get a grip on because I couldn't and wouldn't give her up without a fight. "I could help."

Her face changed and pinched, then went peaceful.

Then pinched again. She was battling herself. Over me. "Ryder."

No. Not this time. "Just think about it? Please?" Yeah. I'd beg. And it wouldn't be the last time. But right now, I had something to take care of.

I drove to Dad's office. Waited in the lobby like I wasn't the son of the man whose name was on the door. Then I waited some more. He had clients. I got it. But even knowing that didn't make the waiting any easier. But nothing was more important to me than this. So, if it took all day, that was exactly how long I'd wait.

One Decade Ago

I STARED AT MY DAD. And at the woman who couldn't have been more than my age. Probably less. Dad didn't even have the courtesy to look guilty. Instead, he nodded to the door, telling me without a word to leave my friend's boat. I stood still and crossed my arms.

"Ryder, I need a moment." Oh, he needed more than that. He needed an entire protection squad because once Mom found out Dad was seeing a woman young enough to be his daughter, she was going to kill him. Probably with her bare hands. And he'd deserve it. It wasn't often I was on Mom's side, but today, what choice did I have? He was wrong.

"I'll wait on the deck." Because no way in hell was I leaving here until I knew exactly what the hell was going on, who he thought he was, and what the fuck he thought he was doing.

It took a good thirty more minutes for him to appear and I didn't let my mind go to what he might've been doing in that time. I didn't need to know. But he appeared beside me at the stern of the boat. "I should explain."

"Yeah." He was and had always been big with the obvious.

At least he had the decency to look ashamed. But under that, I didn't see much in the way of feeling. "I'm sorry for what you saw."

"Is she gone?" Not that it mattered, but with everything that had happened over the last few days, I didn't need someone around documenting this conversation for the newspapers, and I trusted no one. Except Dad, but that was done now, too.

He nodded and held out a beer. I shook my head. This wasn't a have a drink with Dad kind of moment. If I was anyone else, or someone who hadn't been responsible for dragging his parents and himself through the dirtiest parts of the gutter in the last few days and weeks, I probably would've been freaked out, crazed by what I'd seen. But I was Ryder Kennedy, ringleader of the Glouster Four, a man with no home, no friends, no one to lean on but my dad. I sighed and waited for whatever excuse he was going to make. Probably something in the "Mom's a cold fish" category.

"I'm sorry you saw all of that, son." But he hadn't said he was sorry he'd done it. Noted.

Jesus, frozen fish or not, Mom was going to kill him.

She was already on a warpath with me in her sights. For one wild second, I gave him the benefit of the doubt—the idea that he'd done this to distract Mom from hating me so badly. Then reality sank back in. He'd done this because he'd wanted to get laid, to have some sweet young thing look up at him and worship at his belt buckle. Worship him in a way that my mother never had and never would.

"How long have you been cheating on Mom with that… girl?" I wasn't trying to think of a bad name for her. I wanted to convey to him how young she was and how awful he looked.

"With this one?"

Oh, Lord. There was more than one. "Dad." I raked my hands through my hair and turned away as disappointment ached inside of me. Divorce was better than deception. Especially deception that would set her off like one of those bombs that leveled everything around it.

"Look, I'm not going to explain this to you because… she's your mother and I'm your father and we have our own life that has nothing to do with you."

Nothing to do with me? He had to be kidding. "You brought this to my doorstep. To my friend's boat." Which we were currently breaking about ten laws by being aboard because of the line of yellow police tape and the broken seal on the door that lead to the bedroom below deck.

But more than to my friend's boat. And often. Oh, shit. To my room at the frat house. That was why he'd been "dropping off money" so often lately. I felt stupid. I'd actually believed he'd convinced Mom I was working hard and doing well. He'd just needed the excuse to come to campus and the frat house.

He didn't speak, only continued to sip intermittently from his bottle of beer.

"Dad…"

He set the bottle down. "Ryder, this is between your mother and me. I hope I can count on your discretion. And in return, I'll continue to bring money from your account as often as I can." Something about my dad asking me to lie for him made my stomach churn.

I couldn't do it. No matter what she was or wasn't, she was my mom. She'd given birth to me. Loved to talk about the hours of labor and the scar giving birth to me had left behind. And by *talk*, I meant complain and throw up to me, but still.

"Can I count on you, son?" He dropped a hand on my shoulder. A meaningful squeeze. An earnest look. Fuck. He was my dad.

I nodded, but the whole thing made me sick. My skin was too tight for my body and my mind too small to hold everything I knew. But I would lie for him because as much as she was my mom, he was my dad. He was the guy who'd kept the monsters from under my bed and the one who taught me how to throw a football. He was the guy who protected me from Mom's wrath when I was a kid and shielded me from as much as he could as I got older. I owed him this.

"But you have to stop, Dad. If she finds out…"

He chuckled. "Divorce would embarrass her far more." He sighed. "That's what she worries about. Embarrassment. Having her good name tarnished with the society ladies or in the circles she controls, anyway." The wind had been knocked out of him enough times he knew what mattered to her, learned it in order to protect himself and others—to protect me. Now it was fair that I returned the favor.

13

Reese

*J*ust *think about it.* And I would've been fine, had the great and too beautiful to be resisted Ryder Kennedy not added, *please.* Now *it* was all I could think about. *It* consumed my every waking moment. Especially since he asked if he could come back later on so we could talk about *it,* and I'd swallowed every ounce of pride I'd ever had and nodded like a fool.

Now, I sat across from him, takeout cartons open between us, empty plates beside unused silverware at the appropriate place settings.

"Thanks for dinner." I could be gracious. Even if I sounded constipated.

He nodded. "No problem. I thought you might be hungry."

Wow. Small talk was not our strong suit. I tapped my finger against the end of my fork. Not the business end so it didn't do more than make a tinking sound against my nail. A distraction. Not a good one, though.

"Did you get everything accomplished you wanted to?" He hadn't shared his plans with me, but he had left quickly enough.

"No. Today goes down as a failure for me." He didn't elaborate. Just watched my finger tink tink tink against the silverware. I didn't really notice the level of annoyance the sound induced until he covered my hand with his. "How was your day?"

I couldn't remember the last time someone had asked me that. The last time anyone had cared. Even Mom, a very compassionate person who could read me before I spoke, never asked about my day unless she sensed something was wrong.

"It was…okay." Did he really want to know that Mom's washing machine had shot craps and I'd sat on the floor in the basement for an hour bawling because her old Maytag finally gave up and she would've mourned it so I felt I had to also? Or about the ham and cheese sandwich I'd coupled with Doritos and added to a citrus soda for lunch? Maybe the bag of chocolate candies I'd found and eaten during a who's the daddy kind of talk show? Probably not.

"Did you happen to talk to the bank?"

I flipped my gaze up. Maybe I should have called Larry at First Federal but I couldn't bring myself to make a decision. Even though I knew time was…important. "No."

He nodded and sat back. "So, you're giving up the house." It wasn't a question, so I didn't answer. I watched him instead. His grip on the armrests of the chair. His eyes, flicking back and forth over the top of the table. The vein throbbing in his temple. The slight nod as he shoved his chair back and stood, walked out the patio door to stand on the back deck. Mom's beat-up barbecue grill sat against the rail, leaking ash from a hole in the bottom with every step he took.

After a few steps, he stopped, crossed his arms, and stared at the backyard. The door stood open behind him and the sun put him in silhouette. Silhouette Ryder was as attractive as fully-lit, half-darkened, and lit-by-candle Ryder.

I stood and walked to stand just behind him, close enough I could smell his cologne and feel the heat radiating off him. And because he made me weak and pathetic, I wrapped my arms around his waist and laid my cheek against his shoulder blade.

Nothing about hugging Ryder Kennedy was bad. Every ridge and valley of his body, the warmth, the thump of his heart, every breath that rustled his shirt felt…right under my hand. "Ryder…" I wanted him again. Like maybe I could indulge enough to hold me over when I went back to California and tried to resume my normal life.

He covered my hands with his but didn't turn and so I might've misheard his whisper, but it certainly sounded like, "I don't want you to go back to California."

I kissed his spine, just below the nape of his neck. "I know." But I didn't have a job. Or the money to save the house from foreclosure. Maybe not even the will to come back and face falling back into the desperation and need I'd felt before and that was creeping back into my blood with every minute I was here.

Finally, he turned, pulled me close, stroked my throat with his thumb, and held me with his other arm. "So, we're enjoying now?"

I grinned up at him. "God, I hope so." My fingers tangled in his hair, and I tugged him down for a kiss. Soft, Tentative. Waiting for him to take it over, and when he didn't, I pushed harder. Swiped my tongue over his lips. And this time, when I ground my hips against his and he didn't respond, I was the one begging. "Please, Ryder."

Whether it was the softness of my voice, the plea in my tone, or the flex of our relationship muscles, it didn't matter. He used his arm to lift me off my feet and hold me against him, to deepen our kiss with his body. If I had to pick my favorite of all his special skills, this was the one— my number one draft pick.

His low groan, husky and deep, vibrated through me, and there wasn't a better sound I'd ever heard. My blood burned with need. My body tingled for more.

"Reese."

I pulled him inside because Mom's neighbors didn't need to know or see firsthand what was about to happen if I had my way about things. Then it was all him. Urgent. Frantic. Eager. So hot I could hardly breathe. His hands slipped under the hem of my shirt, pushing it up as he glided along my skin, teasing me with his touch and the air and the perfect set of lips trailing along my throat.

My shirt landed on the kitchen counter. I kicked off my shoes on the way to the bedroom. When we stopped against the wall and he lifted me again, this time I wrapped my legs around him, and bucked my hips enough to rub my aching core against his cock.

Every step toward the bedroom and every kiss built the pressure inside of me. I didn't have the time or patience to wait for foreplay. Not today. Not now. As soon as he cleared the bedroom door, I slid down his body to stand on the floor, then pushed him back toward the bed until the backs of his legs hit the mattress. Then it was all sliding down the jeans—his and mine, kicking mine away—and climbing on top of him. This time, we were condom care-ful, and I held back for as long as I could, adjusting my pace and my breathing and my focus on drawing out the pleasure for both of us.

Until finally, he flipped me onto my back and drove into me with power and passion and determination that made my body explode. And when his body went rigid and his breath held, when he shuddered and closed his eyes, I fell into the feeling of the moment. "Oh, God, Ryder."

"Mmm." He collapsed on me for a second, then rolled off onto his back and flung his arms over his face. "You make me weak."

The illusion of my feminine power washed over me. I clung to it until it disappeared. Then I chuckled. "I think I'm the one in need of oxygen."

He kissed my forehead, stood, and walked to the bath-room. The water ran, steam rolled into the bedroom, and he came along with it, lifted me from the bed, and a moment later, lowered me into a steaming tub. Then he climbed in behind me, and after some awkward jostling and moving back and forth, sloshing water over the sides of the old claw foot, I leaned back against him.

Ryder. A tub of oil-scented water. Steam rising. This was what heaven had to be like.

The light flickered and went out. Another reason to let the house go. The wiring was ancient. Probably installed by Benjamin Franklin himself and would cost me thousands to replace.

"Could just be a bulb."

But it wasn't. Not with my luck. And I wasn't going to let it bother me. Not until this water and the man behind me both cooled.

"Could be I don't care." I let my head fall back onto his shoulder and enjoyed the kiss he pressed against my temple.

"You want to just sit here in the dark?"

"Like I'm keeping my eyes open anyway." Nothing was more relaxing than the spot I was in, lights or not, but my stomach growled. I'd ignored our takeout. Still, I didn't move. This was the place I wanted to be and the man I wanted to be with. For the next couple days, anyway.

One Decade Ago

WHY I'D THOUGHT a new look would erase all those old habits—shying away, not asking for what I wanted, not holding my head up high—made no sense.

I still had to walk or drive past the Alpha house every day, new hair and clothes or not. Fraternity Road was directly between campus and my place to live. Beth hadn't been around much. Had a new boyfriend and a new cause with her revenge against the Alphas. And she hated my new look. Hated everything about the way I'd changed myself.

So I was dealing with all of this alone and it was too much. Too much not to indulge in a few drinks, anyway. Besides, with the way I looked these days, people expected me to either be dancing on top of the bar or slinging drinks from behind it. Made sense for me to spend some time soaking up that atmosphere.

It was two o'clock on a Tuesday afternoon. I belonged in Economics class sitting behind the nervous laugher who punctuated his notes with an involuntary chuckle. But instead, I sidled up to the bar and smiled at the bartender. He was young, probably my age, also probably a Monday, Wednesday, and Friday class taker.

"What can I get for you?"

I wanted to drink something as badass as my new look, but I didn't know what to order. "Surprise me."

He looked me up and down. Well what he could see anyway-from my hair to my chest, then settled on my chest before he grinned. "I got you."

He disappeared down the bar then came back with a long, tall glass with an umbrella sticking over the rim on one side, pineapple on the other, and an orange slice halfway down the frozen concoction.

"Wow. That's…tall."

"Try it."

I took a sip, let it sit on my tongue and melt just a little so I could enjoy every tropic burst of flavor. "This is like a party in my mouth. Well done."

He laughed and moved down the bar as someone slid into the seat beside me. He gave the bartender his order—Jack and Coke sounded so smooth the way he said it—then sat back and folded his hands over his midsection. I felt him watching me, like a hand on my back. And I almost checked to see if there was one there or if it was in my imagination.

Finally, he moved to rest his arm against the bar and to make his stare more blatant. "Do I know you?"

Yeah, he did. Not only did Jameson King not know a stranger, Ryder had introduced us before. I didn't answer but took another long drink of my beverage and suffered an ice-cream headache. I held my forehead, and he chuckled.

"Hard to look cool when you have the same affliction a six-year-old gets from eating her pushup pop." I chuckled, still massaging my temples.

"You look fine." His voice was as smooth as butter. Like they all—the Alpha I knew anyway—took a class on how to sound like every word just rolled off their tongues.

I smiled. "Mm. What girl doesn't want to look *fine*?"

"Why don't you let me buy you a real drink?" He nodded to the headache maker. "Kiddie cocktails aren't gonna do the job."

"Who said I'm here to get drunk?" Although it was two o'clock on a Tuesday afternoon. If that didn't say desperation drinking, not much else would.

He cocked his head. "Well, if not, you can sit with me while I do." Like that was going to happen.

The temptation to ask him about Ryder loomed large between us, and the clinking ice in my new drink, the warm burn of the whisky, the smoldering look I didn't think Jameson could control, faded my resolve. And by my third drink, I was pouring out my heart.

"I knew I knew you." He smiled as soon as I mentioned Ryder's name. "You're the nun."

"Not anymore." I held out my leg and showed him my ankle tattoo—a very tasteful pair of ballet shoes being sliced by a blood-dripping knife. The guy who'd done it made it look like the knife had sliced a three-dimensional gash in my calf before attacking the shoes.

He took my calf in his giant hand and pulled it up at the same time he bent. If he looked left, he would have a view of my panties and whatever the thin strip of fabric didn't manage to hide, but he kept his gaze trained on my tattoo. "Wow. That's sick."

I could only guess, but the way he said it made sick sound like a good thing, so I smiled. "Thanks."

Then he let go of my leg and rolled up his sleeve, shoving his forearm toward me. "Check this one out." It was in the same three-dimensional style as the "gash" on my leg, but it was a black hole about halfway between his wrist and elbow. Then he lifted the bottom of his shirt and showed me a "bullet hole" inked into the space of his chest just above his heart.

"That's awesome."

As he rolled his sleeve back into place, he gave me a

once-over. "I guess Ryder's the reason for all of this?" He wagged his finger in front of my smoky-lidded face before resuming the fastening of his cuff button.

But the question was all the opening I needed. "Let's call him the inspiration." But it didn't matter what pretty name I gave it, the truth was that as I was, I hadn't been able to look into the mirror anymore without feeling like I'd lost all that made me who I was. It was either reinvent myself or fade away.

Jameson leaned in. "You want to hear something?" When I nodded, and took a drink so he didn't have to look at me, he sighed. "I'm as guilty as Ryder. I made the website."

"I thought all the punishments have been handed down already." The press had made a giant deal of the cops not pursuing criminal charges against any of the boys except Ryder. There were rumors of scholarship losses, and the four of them had been kicked off the football team, which benefited Keaton who'd been signed to a pro team, and didn't much affect Jameson who'd been injured and had a knee brace on his left leg. Finn hadn't been seen at school in a couple days and Felicity was beside herself, but Ryder had a trust fund as big as the college's budget and a job at his parents' firm waiting for him no matter if he had to finish his law degree online at some half-ass law school.

"They were." He nodded. "But no one knows I helped Ryder." He shook his head. "Not even Finn and Keats."

I shrugged. Didn't matter. What was done…done. "Why would you help him with that?"

Now, he shrugged. "You know him. He's Ryder. My best

friend. If he asks, I do. No questions." Such loyalty was hard to find. I hoped Ryder appreciated it.

"He's lucky to have you."

He laughed. "I'd say he was lucky to have you."

I rolled my eyes to keep the tears back because just the mention of my failed relationship with Ryder made me tear up, and drinking while I discussed it certainly wasn't going to turn out better. "That's all over now. "

"Yeah. He was out with Susie last night." I didn't know what he saw on my face, but he started shaking his head almost before he finished talking. "You know…no big deal. I ended up taking her home."

Too much information. And it made me mean. Or maybe *that* was the whisky. "You're actually bragging?" The fucking nerve.

"No!" He shook his head and scoffed. "I brought her home and sat with her. All night. Just sat and talked to her because not all of us are pigs."

"Says the guy who created the website that started the whole mess." Bitterness didn't just heat my blood, it burned in my tone, too.

"Yeah. I know." He motioned for another round. "Hey, Alex. A couple more."

The bartender nodded and made our drinks while I babbled to Jameson. "I loved him, you know? And he… broke me. Like a hammer through a glass window broke me." I shook my head. "Not everything he said to me was bullshit, though. It was…not."

"Nothing he said about you if it made you change who

you are was right, Reese." He looked away from me when Alex sat our drinks down.

"You guys are up to like forty bucks." We'd had four of these each at five bucks each, so Jameson's confusion didn't make much sense.

"You guys have an open tab for the Alphas."

Alex shook his head. "Ryder's card's been turned off for a while now. It's all cash for you guys unless you have a different card you want to use."

Jameson's skin turned red, dangerous, stroke red. Didn't take a genius. He didn't have any money. "I got this."

I pulled a couple twenties from my bag and tossed them onto the counter. "You can get us next time we run into each other." I couldn't be sure he heard me. He honestly looked as if he wasn't seeing or hearing anything and it had nothing to do with the watered-down whisky we'd been drinking. "Are you okay?" I laid a hand on his shoulder then cupped his bearded cheek. "Jameson?"

"Oh shit. This really is the end." It was as if he'd just realized how on the wrong side of things he'd become. "I can't pay you back."

"I don't need..."

"Unless you want me to do your homework or I could have sex with you for the money..." He shook his head. "I don't have a job or money or...fuck." He went from red to green. I'd seen that look before. A look that required fast action.

I pushed away from the bar and pulled him from his stool, led him outside and around the building, waited for him to throw up the twenty dollars worth of alcohol we'd drank then handed him a wet-wipe packet I'd kept from a rib place I'd stopped at the other day after shopping for some more comfortable boots.

"Thanks." When I nodded, he looked down and leaned a shoulder against the building. "You're way too good for him." His eyes filled with tears. "I'm so screwed, Reese. What am I going to do?"

I didn't have an answer, but I had a shoulder. I pulled him close and let him crowd me against the building as he cried it out into my hair and my throat. Then his lips brushed my neck and his hands circled my waist—Jesus, this guy had big hands—and pulled me closer to him. I pushed him back. There wasn't time to panic because he was too big, too strong. I gave him a shove anyway and prayed he would be off balance enough or smart enough to fall back. "Come on, Jameson."

He took a full step back and held up his hands like I'd forced his surrender. "I'm sorry."

"You took a shot. It didn't work out. We'll pretend…it didn't happen." I nodded, swallowing back the fear. Instead, I held out my hand. "Come on. We need to get you home. Where are you staying?"

He walked three steps then took a break like he wasn't used to two-a-day practices and running wind sprints. "In my mom's fucking basement. How pathetic is that?"

"It could be worse." Homelessness. Hunger. Instead, he had a warm bed to fall into and a dry place to live.

He nodded and started walking again, this time pulling me around the side of the building to the parking lot. "You know what? He doesn't deserve you." I didn't want to encourage more intimate behavior that would give him the idea I was up for more than getting us both home safely, so I didn't answer. "He shouldn't have broke your heart."

This time, I shrugged. "Yours either."

"I deserve it. You don't." He closed his eyes and swayed then opened them up again with a smile. "Anytime you want to get back at him…" He grinned and shot me the finger guns along with a wink then stumbled toward the bus shelter.

I turned in the opposite direction, toward the apartment, and I walked all the way there, ignoring the do not disturb bra hanging on the door. It was five blocks from the bar and I needed to use the bathroom. Beth could've had a do not disturb tiger guarding the door and I would've walked right in past it.

But I didn't make it three feet before I saw the clothes strewn from the front door to the sofa where she was on the couch with a guy I would've recognized anywhere, a guy who thirty years ago was probably his own version of the big man on campus, but the alcohol in my blood and the urge to pee stopped me from investigating further.

14

Ryder

At some point, I was going to have to go back and try again to see my Dad, but Mom had a blockade so big protecting him from me, that I couldn't get through. No forgive or forget in her game. Obviously. But she underestimated how much this meant to me. How far Dad's help would go with what I needed.

I spent the afternoon in the lobby. Again. Saw Mom pass from one side of the building to the other—and not by accident either. Nothing happened by accident. Not with her. She knew I was there. She knew I'd see her on the inside while I waited outside the glass doors. Hell, she probably even knew what I wanted to say to Dad before I figured it out.

Around four, I finally figured he wasn't coming out. And no way was I getting in. So, I went to the parking garage, marveling at the lack of security that allowed me to walk through the gate straight to Dad's car—a sportscar that had all the flash and bang of a midlife crisis. Well, at least I knew he was there.

When he finally walked out, it was after six, and Mom was long gone. She had a Monday Massage which meant I had about ten minutes to talk to him before he went to his Monday night mistress, not to be confused with his Tuesday afternoon Tootsie, his Wednesday whatever, Thursday something or other, etcetera, etcetera.

"Hey, Dad." I pushed off the wall and met him at his car door. "I know you're in a big hurry, but I need to talk to you."

"I tried to get a note out to you, but no one wants to go against your mother."

I shrugged. That was okay. I couldn't very well expect Dad to grow a pair now when he hadn't in thirty years. But I could expect him to help me out. Whether or not those expectations were worthy would remain to be seen. "I need money, Dad. And not the hundred here and there you've been giving me."

He shook his head, eyes wide. "She's never going to go for that."

No shit. "I don't want your money. Or hers. I want you to sign a loan with me at the bank. Use your name to get me enough to buy a house, get on my feet."

His mouth twisted from one side to the other. "Ry, I don't know. What if you can't pay it back? She'd have a fucking cow."

"You work at that law firm, too, Dad. The money is half yours." And he knew what I'd done for him, and even though I never mentioned it, I would now if necessary. He knew that, too. At least he should have.

Dad shook his head. "It's easier not to fight with her."

Well, didn't I know that? But I was his kid. "You fight this hard for your clients? Or just your son?" The bitter anger probably didn't help my cause, but he'd sat back for a decade and let her punish me over and over again while I protected him and his secrets from her.

"Ry..." He reached for his door handle as if he was going to climb in his car and zoom away, as if I didn't know where he worked and lived and couldn't do all of this again tomorrow.

"Dad, please." I might as well have been him for all the begging I'd had to do these days. But this was too important for me to let him say no. "Please, help me. I'll never ask again. Hell, you'll never see me again if that's what you want."

It took a minute. Several, actually, before he nodded. "I'll call Ed tonight and have him draw up the papers. Go find a house."

I told him what I wanted, even why it was important, then gave him the number to the bank whose envelope I'd found in the desk when I was looking for a pen.

"You love her?"

Of course, I did. And I took the bus back to her place, all the while grinning like an idiot because knowing I was in love with her was almost as happiness-inducing as actually being in love with her. The only thing better was the kiss she laid on me when I walked in her door.

"Hello to you, too." I held her against me and looked

down while she looked up. The number of boxes sitting in the corner of the living room had multiplied today and when she led me to the kitchen, all the what-nots and wall hangings that had made it homey and lived in were gone. The cabinets with their glass fronts were all empty and parts of the counter that hadn't seen daylight in years now shined under the fluorescent light overhead. "You've been busy."

She grinned. "Making hay while the sun shines so I can roll around in it all night with you."

I didn't want to let her eagerness to pack bother me. Didn't want to spend whatever time we had together with a minute of unhappiness, but neither did I want to make her leaving me easy. But I was too happy to see her after being away all day and the last thing I wanted was to fight. Instead, I pasted a smile on and lowered my head. "Is it night yet?"

The first kiss of the day was always my favorite. She'd been asleep this morning when I left, so the eight a.m. kiss on her cheek didn't count. But this one did and I made sure. On a scale of one to ten, it hit a solid twelve. She pushed her hands through my hair and curled them in and out against my scalp.

"You're beautiful." I wanted to tell her every minute of every single day. The same as I wanted to kiss her every minute. Touch her. Hold her. Talk to her.

"Just shut up and kiss me."

I wasn't one to argue. Not with an order like that, anyway. One kiss led to another and another and a couple more before we pulled apart. "Should we order a pizza?"

My account wasn't looking good and I hadn't worked all week. "I could cook."

She bent her knees and almost knelt in front of me and my eyes automatically rolled back. But she blazed a trail of kisses up from my belly button to my left nipple then the right. She flicked her tongue over each one then smiled up at me when I shucked the shirt. "That's what I'm talking about."

"Packing turns you on?" Because it would've completely turned me off, except she was really persistent. Kissing my throat, her leg hiked over my hip, her warm heat against my dick.

"Thinking about you while I'm packing turns me on." She grinned and pulled my head down so that her lips were at the shell of my ear. "Ask me what I was thinking about."

Her breath warmed every cell in my body and my dick —already hard enough to cut glass—twitched. I wanted to talk to her, to make her understand how important she was to me and the plan I had for us, but…that tongue flicked out and traced my ear down to the lobe that she pulled between her teeth while she continued rubbing her pussy against my cock, moaning randomly while I palmed her breast through her shirt then shoved it out of the way along with her bra so I could feel her skin, tease her nipple until it was as hard as my dick.

Before I could react to much, she shoved my jeans down, then her sweats and she turned to lean across the counter, her back and that luscious ass of hers pointed toward me. Oh, God. This woman.

"Come on, baby." Her short breaths huffed out between

the words as she reached behind her to try to pull me in. I took a condom from my pants pocket—I'd started keeping one there for these kinds of occasions—rolled it on then drove into her. She cried out and wrapped her arm behind us, to grab a handful of my ass.

We were a tangle of breaths, of hands and legs, of moans and sweat. I needed to tell her what I'd done today, but right now, I just wanted to hear her cry out, to feel her body tighten around mine, to love her in every way I knew how.

She stiffened, straightened and moved against me, moaned and cried out, pushed against me so I was in as deep as I could go. And it was all too much. All enough to make my body respond, to shatter any hint of self-control I might've been clinging to. I shattered, blew apart, and collapsed.

There was something about this woman. She shredded my resolve to stay tough, to be able to let her go. She gave me hope whether she meant to or not. But she was hell-bent on leaving. And now, standing in the kitchen with my pants around my ankles, I was rethinking everything about today. She didn't want to stay here. She wanted her life back. Wouldn't have even come home to Glouster had her mom not passed away. And now, I'd bought her house. Fuck. What was I thinking?

"What's wrong?" She turned to look at me as I got rid of the condom and yanked my pants up.

"Nothing." I shook my head, ears burning, and I couldn't look at her. No way could I hide my stupidity from her. "I'm great."

Once we were all put back together, she slapped her hands together and rubbed them back and forth. "I'm going to order pizza. My treat."

For the first time, it really sank in. She didn't want to be here. Wanted to go back to her life, the one without me in it. Not that she hadn't told me but seeing how dedicated she'd been in her packing today only reinforced what I'd been too stubborn to hear.

My guts ached and I was about two minutes from throwing up. Losing her once had almost killed me. Oh, God. I couldn't do this again. "I should go." I hadn't been home in days. Not that I had a reason to go home. No plants to water or pets to feed, and the thought of leaving her, until now, left a hole in me. Now it seemed the only thing that would heal the pain rocketing through my blood.

"What?" She glanced at me, frowning, eyes narrow. Then, as quickly as she reacted, she erased it all. "Yeah." She nodded all the way to the door. "Will I see you tomorrow?" I didn't answer. "You know, I should probably concentrate on getting this all taken care of anyway, so…" And she held out her hand. Her fucking hand. "It's been…great catching up with you." Her tongue clicked against her teeth and she blew out a breath.

"Catching up. Yeah." My heart ached, like it had taken an electrical shock and hadn't quite snapped back into business yet. I held onto her hand a second too long, lingered like an idiot until one of us—probably her—pulled away.

I walked to the door, still slow, still hovering like I

was expecting her to ask me to stay. Even when I knew she wouldn't. Even when there was no doubt this was over.

When I twisted the knob on the front door, she laid her hand over my spine. "Thanks for…everything."

I didn't speak because breaking down and crying like a baby was the last thing I wanted to do. Especially in front of her. The least I could do was wait for the cross-town bus for that.

One Decade Ago

DAD DROPPED a hand on my shoulder. "Everything is finished now. You have restitution to pay and weekends in jail for a few months."

I could accept my part in all of this. I nodded. "Okay." I didn't want to ask, but I couldn't not know. It wasn't as much about the money as everyone seemed to think, either. "Is Mom…?"

He shook his head. "She's not coming. And she's made it so that you can't get any more money out of your trust fund until you're thirty-five." He cleared his throat. "Also, she had Michael pick up your truck."

No. This couldn't be happening. "Dad, is there anything you can do?" This was my whole life. My everything. I'd already lost any hope I ever had of becoming a lawyer. Now I had no car, no money, nowhere to live. And I'd lost my family.

"I wish I could help, son." He stared at me as if he was

waiting for me to say it was okay. It wasn't okay. Nothing about this was okay. Especially since…

"I know what you're doing. What you have been doing with Beth and Susie." It was shitty and wrong, one of those last-ditch things I should've kept quiet. But I was desperate. "If Mom finds out…"

"Ryder." I shrunk from his disappointment. I didn't know which code of his—Guy Code or Father/Son Code—I'd violated, but neither did I care. He'd violated the Children First doctrine of good parenting. Mom always violated that rule, but that was why I counted on Dad. All that innocence shriveled.

"Dad, please." But he opened his wallet, pulled out all the money inside—two-hundred and ninety-three dollars—and turned to walk back to his car.

I was angry and alone. I had no one to call. No one in the world who would care if I was dead in a ditch.

I looked at the money in my hand. Counted it. Shoved it into my wallet. It was going to be cold soon. I had to figure out something.

I went to the office supply store for envelopes and stamps then the public library where I printed out eleven dollars of resumes. I scanned copies of today's paper and sent off all the resumes, then I stuck around for a while and applied for every job I could find online.

Of course, it took me a week to figure out that she'd shut off my phone, and I'd wasted all the money on the resumes and supplies. Now, not only did I have no one to call, I had no way to call.

I walked into The Diner, a campus hangout, and felt

every eye in the place shift to look at me. To stare. Judging me. Holding me accountable. Fuck. If only they knew. I ordered a cup of coffee and a cup of soup—trying to stretch that money as far as I could—then sat at the counter and watched the place implode. The waitress couldn't keep up and the cook sent out three orders of burned pancakes.

The waitress sloshed my soup across the counter, then sighed. "I'll get you a new one."

I'd spent three days sleeping in the gazebo at the park, but tonight, the temperature was supposed to drop. So, I did what I had to do. I walked behind the counter, into the kitchen, and started working. Pitching in. "Tell me what you need."

The cook had tickets piled on the table and food on plates that needed other food added. He needed to organize this mess, take a breath, get himself under control, then find a method.

And an hour later, I'd done it. Things might not have been perfect, but the line of tickets was cleared, no one sent anything back, and I had a job.

I went back to the front with a plate of eggs and bacon. This was the first solid food I'd had since before Dad told me I'd been cut off, and I wanted to savor every bite, but I couldn't. I was starving.

The guy—Jack, the cook—stood across the counter from me. "Thanks, man. And like I said, if you want to come in tomorrow, around eleven, you can work with me through lunch and then supper, too."

I nodded, still shoveling in the food. I never realized

until that moment how much I'd taken the ability to order a burger and fries or a steak omelet anytime I wanted for granted. "Thanks."

"If you want to come back in tonight, you can work through dinner." He chuckled. "Doesn't pay much, but you can eat here. Pick up any shift you want. We're always busy." I nodded still eating. "We open at six, so we start prep at four-thirty. Switch over at ten, but we serve break-fast all day." He continued filling me in. But it didn't matter if he said I had to swim naked through the grease trap. This job meant I could eat again. Like a human being. Now all I had to do was find a place to live.

And no harm in asking around.

Jack chuckled. "I have a room. It's not much. But if you kick in a little rent..." He shrugged.

Weird? Yeah. As a measure of last resort, in the arena of what other choice did I have, at the intersection of tired of sleeping in the park and maybe this was my bounce back, I leaped at the chance of an indoor place to stay.

15

Reese

"Someone bought the house?" I clutched the phone tighter. Until this moment, I hadn't been dead set on my plan to let the house go. But Jerry from the bank was on the phone and it seemed the choice was out of my hands. Dammit.

He explained the short sale and what it meant and that the new owner was more than willing to give me as much time as I needed to clear the place out. Would probably even be willing to rent the place to me.

I looked at the sofa, a spot where Ryder and I had…now piled high with boxes. Then the chair…also a place where…also piled with boxes. The counter. The kitchen table. The hallway carpet. Boxes. Boxes. Boxes. And memories of Ryder.

Funny. I was in Mom's house, and I had more memories of Ryder and me than I had of Mom and me. Or that was how it seemed.

"Thanks, Jerry. But I have the mover's scheduled for Monday, so I'll drop the keys off with you, then." I hung up before he could answer. "I'll be damned." Now that the choice was out of my hands, it upset me more than I could understand. What if I'd wanted to stay? To buy my mother's house myself?

"Too little, too late, stupid."

I was still holding the phone and could've called my boss to tell him I was coming home. But I didn't. Not because I wasn't coming home, but I still had to book a flight, had to make sure everything got shipped…I sat down on the floor in the middle of the kitchen and crossed my legs.

Loss hit me and I laid back to stare at the ceiling. Wow. It needed a painting. And the wallpaper was torn at the top of the window. The brick above the fireplace was blackened with soot. The window itself needed cleaning. The carpet needed…my mind whirled with the things I would do if I'd been the one who bought the house. It wouldn't have taken much to spruce the place up. Some paint. A good scrub. Maybe replace the carpet with a nice wood laminate.

Didn't matter now. I didn't have a choice. Someone had bought the house out from under me.

And if that was the only thing bothering me, maybe I would've been okay. Maybe my eyes wouldn't have pooled with new tears. Maybe I wouldn't have laid on the floor picturing me and Ryder here, lying on the sofa watching

TV together or eating dinner on the back deck, or planting flowers around the tree in the front yard.

It was ten years ago the last time I had thoughts like these, the last time I saw my future with someone else in it. I couldn't be sure if it was a coincidence that both times it was Ryder in those fantasies or if the fantasies were because it was Ryder. All I knew for sure was that the fantasies were the same, and they all had Ryder as the star.

The door opened and Avery and Felicity walked in. Considering a couple days ago, Felicity had come in and caught us, I should've probably instituted the knock twice rule but since I was heading home soon, there really wasn't much point.

"Are you home?" Felicity walked toward the back of the house, calling out while Avery breezed past me into the kitchen. They couldn't see me over the boxes stacked on all the available surfaces.

"Down here." I waved an arm but didn't sit up. "Unless you have wine, go home."

Felicity peeked her head around the wall of cardboard. "What are you doing?"

"Moping." Not much point to lying.

My friends walked around and sat next to one another beside my prone body. "What's wrong, grasshopper? Is your boy toy being more boy and less toy?" She nudged Avery then nodded at me. "I hate when Finn is like that."

I threw my hands up but didn't answer.

"Avery has some gossip." She rolled her eyes. "You know professors know all the best stuff." When I didn't move, she tugged my arm. "Come on. Sit up. This is too juicy to lay down for."

I dragged myself into a seated position, a mopey, back-curved, chin on fist on knee, legs crossed, eyes down mopey position.

"Did somebody die?" Avery swiped my hair away so she could see my face.

"I'm going home. They sold the house." Saying it out loud made it real. Hurt.

"Wasn't that the plan all along?" Felicity looked at Avery then they both stared at me.

"Yes. I just didn't expect…"

Felicity nodded. "Didn't expect Ryder?" I'd been away for a very long time, and we hadn't really been all that close before I left, but they knew me. So well. Maybe because they'd been where I am—in love with one of the Alphas that we shouldn't have even liked.

I nodded. "Yeah. Or that I might…want to stay here." Might want to was such an understatement. I wanted to buy this house, live in it. Probably with Ryder. And another understatement for my collection. Not that I wanted to think about that one.

"You should!"

"You totally should." There was nodding and planning, redecorating and celebrating advice while my head shifted back and forth between them. It was like a tennis match with my life as the ball.

"They sold the house, guys."

"It's not the only house for sale in Glouster." Avery shrugged one shoulder as if it didn't matter whether I lived in this house or a different one. And it probably didn't but…why make a lateral move to continue to live alone?

"I don't have a job here."

"And only California needs cops." Felicity threw in an eye roll and I chuckled and shook my head. This was my whole life we were uprooting, and she was diminishing the importance of my decision to an eye roll.

"It would cost a lot to move across the country."

"I heard private security pays bank, and I happen to know…someone who needs new private security." She nudged Avery. "Which brings me around to my gossip."

I sighed. Now we weren't going to get back around to me until I heard this week's version of the Glouster Entertainment News. "What is it?"

She looked at Avery and nodded. A look passed between them. "Ryder's folks are getting divorced. It's a whole thing." She tucked her hair behind her ear and blew out a breath. "Word on the street"—translation: from a bunch of college coeds who should be more concerned about their grades—"is that Mrs. Kennedy found out something about Mr. Kennedy that didn't sit well. Something so big, she just couldn't forgive."

I loved Avery, but I could've done without added drama. "Like what?"

"You're really not going to believe it." They looked at each other again. "I can't believe it." She shrugged a shoulder. Hemming and hawing. "It doesn't change what they did. Except Ryder."

Now I perked up. "What are you talking about?"

She gulped and sat up straighter. "Well, it seems that

back in the day when the Glouster Four was being crucified by Beth Cooper in the press, she was getting down with none other than Ryder's dad."

Oh, shit. "Oh, shit."

Avery nodded and Felicity picked the story up. "At the boat. The frat house. That big old mansion of theirs. If you would've married Ryder, she would've ended up as your mother-in-law. Because now, they're getting married."

I ignored everything else she'd said because self-preservation required it. "He's already married." Not to point out the obvious, but his current marriage wasn't likely to be one he could just walk away from for Beth Cooper.

"Not for long. Apparently, and I have no confirmed reports about this part, but apparently, he skimmed off of client accounts. A lot of money, and it's going to take the entire family fucking fortune to pay that shit back. She's broke as a joke and he's on the run with roving reporter Beth Cooper." She shrugged and smug-smiled. "And that's not all."

Couldn't have happened to a nicer lady than Mrs. Kennedy. "When did all this happen?" I thought of Ryder. These were the people who'd abandoned him, who'd left him to live in the best way he could find without any thought that they'd pampered him all his life and left him without too many real life skills. Still, he'd managed, but that wasn't the point. And their marital issues weren't really a source for celebration, but I was kind of glad that old bat was getting hers.

"I guess she found out recently, but...it gets better." Avery smiled again. "Ryder didn't upload the videos."

"What?" I tilted my head. I couldn't have heard her correctly. He'd admitted it. Taken all the blame for it. Paid the restitution determined by the court. "What did you say?"

"Oh yeah. Ryder's dad was at the frat house getting his freak on with Beth Cooper—wasn't she your roommate in college? Anyway, getting his freak on. And afterward, he was hanging around waiting for Ryder to give him the weekly allowance, and he wanted to look at his bank account. He opened the laptop and found the videos. Videos of him and Beth. And he was trying to delete them, but he ended up posting the whole folder to the website that Ryder set up to use to make money off the pledges. So Ryder isn't wholly innocent." Apparently, it was important that I knew that. "But his dad is the one who posted the videos."

"Holy crap." It didn't absolve him from the impact he'd caused by taking the videos in the first place. Still, he shouldn't have kept the videos he did. I flipped back and forth. He'd been punished. So much. When would it be enough?

And this was so much to process. And no one brought wine.

One Decade Ago

I STARED INTO HER EYES. This wasn't the Beth Cooper who'd been my friend since...I couldn't remember a time she wasn't my friend. It had always been me and Beth. Beth and me. But now…

She adjusted her shirt and pulled her cardigan tighter around her. Her yoga pants were inside out and it didn't take a genius to know she'd pulled them on in a big hurry. "Who's in there, Beth?"

For the last few months, she'd been sketchy about so many things. Sneaking men or maybe just the one man in and out of the house at all hours of the day and night. "Just a guy."

It really wasn't my business except I was losing a lot of sleep listening to her get her head banged against the headboard every night. I shook my head and walked back into my bedroom. She was an adult. Same as I was.

But I was worried. And that was why when I heard her bedroom door squeak open, I opened mine a crack and peeked out. And my heart broke. She wasn't kissing just anyone. She was kissing Ryder freaking Kennedy. My Ryder.

She'd been leading the crusade against him for months. And months. While I tried not to hold it against her. Tried not to remind her that she'd crawled into bed with him, that the video didn't show any force despite what spin she put on the day's story.

But now, she'd crossed the line. Broke the unwritten rule. Traded on our friendship so she could get off at an inappropriate decibel. Bitch.

I waited until he was gone, because no man was worth that humiliation, then flung my door open. "Really, Beth?

Really?!" My blood burned. "You're fucking Ryder? My Ryder?"

She held out her hand like she was approaching a wild animal. "You have to let me—"

"Explain? Explain how you ask for his head on a spike for months and now you're fucking him in the bedroom next to mine? I think I've heard enough from you." This was too much. I had to get out now. Had to decide how much this bothered me so I could decide if I hated her forever or if I just hated her for now.

I snatched my coat off the rack beside the door, strode past her as if she wasn't standing there with her mouth hanging open, for once speechless or maybe—and even far less likely—quiet because I'd asked it of her. The apartment wasn't big enough for both of us. Not anymore. Not if she could do this to me.

Since I was dressed for it—a tank top/sports bra combo and leggings—I went running. Across campus, past the gym, the science building, the law library, the regular library, Chancellor Hall, the food shops and cafeteria, freshman dorms, to Fraternity Road. I was halfway down the street before it occurred to me where I was. All the houses were lit up. Lights burned in every room down the block, until the Alpha house. It was dark. Even though only four of the boys had been in trouble, the Greek Council revoked this year's permission for the Alpha house to operate and put them on probation for next year. All the jocks had been moved to dorms or rented apartments on their own off campus. Next year, they would start again.

I leaned against a tree, the same one Jameson had found

me hiding behind when I was just trying to get a better look at Ryder. Wow. Things had been so simple back then. Beth had been my best friend. I'd had my one wild night. Gone back for seconds as myself. And still…

No point in thinking of that now.

I ran some more. Through town. Past the butcher shop, the beauty parlor, the ice cream parlor, coffee shop, insurance agency, ladies' clothing boutique, straight back to the apartment. I was sweaty, out of breath, and tired, but I didn't want to see Beth. I just couldn't face her. Or more, I couldn't face what she'd done.

I turned away from my place and headed to Felicity's. We'd only just become friends, but she loved a good story. And tonight, I had one.

16

Ryder

My entire family was on a collision course with implosion. It wasn't ten minutes after Dad called that I got the call from Eduardo, Mom's personal valet. But never did I expect that as soon as I stepped from the car she'd sent to "collect" me, that she would be waiting on the steps, tears streaming, arms wide as I walked toward her.

When she wrapped me in her version of a hug, I tried not to stiffen, but she wasn't really a hugger. Not in my entire life, so I didn't really know how to act or what was going on.

She kept her arm around me and led me inside. When we were in the sitting room, tea poured and cooling in front of us, she scooted closer to me. I watched her from the corner of my eye. Her chin quivered and her hands shook as she brought them to her mouth. "All I can think is what if you would've had kids, or found a woman you loved, or…" Her voice quivered and she brought her fist to her mouth. This sentiment was so out of character, I couldn't…but she'd been through so much in the last few hours—finding out about Dad and Beth Cooper, finding out he'd stolen the family fortune, all the skeletons out of the family closet.

"Mom, it's okay." It wasn't. Even on our best day, the relationship between us was strained. And we hadn't had a best day since I went to my first day of kindergarten and made her an ashtray a month after she quit smoking.

"It wasn't you."

I shook my head. "Some of it was."

"Your father let you accept all the blame, spend forty-three weekends in jail. Pay back all that money." She shook her head and more tears fell. In all my years I'd never seen her cry. Not when my grandparents died or her dog, although I'd always suspected that the little purse puppy was more of an expected possession than a pet. "Did you know what he'd done?"

"Cheating?"

She scoffed. "No. He was never very good at hiding that particular sin against our family." Her tone went dry until I nodded. "Why didn't you tell me he was the one who uploaded those videos?"

I didn't point out that she wouldn't have believed me. Not yet. I really wanted to see where this was going. "I don't know. But I made the videos so…" I shrugged. One sin was as bad as the other.

She looked down and picked up her tea for a drink, set

it down with nary a wobble of cup against saucer, then looked at me again. "He stole your trust fund."

"It wasn't mine anymore anyway."

She sighed. "I know you didn't want it anymore. That was why I found your ransom prank so curious, because even though it was dwindling fast, there was still plenty of money in there. More than you asked for anyway."

My brain hitched on didn't want it anymore. "Hold on. What does *didn't want it anymore* mean?" My stomach ached. I'd never tried to take money from the account. He'd always done it for me. Paid my cards, my bills, my school tuition. I wasn't even sure how to get money out of the account.

She closed her eyes and looked down. "I understood when I came back from Madagascar that you'd wanted to move out, to go away and try to start again. And doing it on your own was…admirable…" She sniffed and I shook my head.

This had to be a joke, but my stomach revolted and shot everything I'd eaten in the last month into a dead spin in my gut. I stood and ran for the bathroom. For ten years, I'd covered for him. Lied for him. Taken the blame for what he'd done. Fuck!

I threw up until there was nothing left. And when I was finished, I took the stairs to my old room. It was just as I'd left it. Oh shit. He kicked me out of my life to keep me away from Mom. I walked in and sat on my bed. I'd spent so many nights sleeping on floors and in that fucking gazebo. And my Dad had let it happen.

"I didn't change anything."

"You didn't kick me out?" I already knew, but I needed to hear her say it.

She walked in and sat beside me. "I was so angry at you. So...disappointed, but I wanted to help you. I pulled the firm's best lawyers to help you..." She laced her fingers through mine and gave me a squeeze. "But I didn't understand why you were so angry at me you would leave."

Oh, God. If my Dad had been standing there, nothing would have stopped me from punching him in the throat. "Fuck." I couldn't stop the tears—some from relief, some from anger, some from pain—or the sobs, or the arms that reached out for my mother.

After a while, I lifted my head, dried my eyes, and looked at her. "Just to clarify, you never kicked me out? Took my truck? Cut off my money?"

She shook her head. "No. He told me you gave it all back and you didn't want our help anymore. You wanted to handle your business without us." She sighed. "I thought it was quite admirable at the time, but when you stopped taking my calls and sending those horrible texts...I never meant to be a bad mother."

"I didn't send any texts. And I never called you..." Well...

Fuck. All along, I'd hated her. Blamed her. But it was Dad. He'd cut me off from her. Kept us away from each other by telling us each the other one was pissed, knowing neither of us would check with the other. Because I knew too much?

"Ryder, I'm so sorry."

So was I.

And then she started laughing. Hysterically. Manically. Until even more tears ran down her cheeks. Along with the crying, I couldn't remember ever seeing her laugh either. I liked it.

"Mom?" I touched her shoulder.

"He stole all my money." She doubled over again. "All of it."

I watched her. At some point, I was going to have to find a phone to call a therapist or psychiatrist, but right now, I wanted to know where she was going with this.

"Mom?"

"It's the irony. Don't you see?" She blew out three big breaths then drew in a deep one before she nodded. "Okay, all these years, I've tolerated your father cheating because he always came home to me. But he only came home so he could figure out how to steal my money." I didn't really see the irony or anything funny about any of this. "He left me with...the only thing that ever mattered to me. After all this time."

"How are you going to live without money?"

She cocked an eyebrow. "Darling, I never put all my eggs in one basket. We're going to be fine." She patted my hand. "And I have jewelry, properties. Things your father couldn't take." She smiled. "And I have you back where you belong. I would happily live in a shack for that."

We still had a lot of things to work out, but we were going to be okay. Because as smart as Dad was, I bet Mom's tech team was smarter and I was also willing to bet that he'd put those accounts in my name.

One Decade Ago

I STARED AT DAD. "She's watching me like a hawk, probably discovered a couple twenties missing from the account." He chuckled but handed over a couple of twenties.

"Thanks, Dad."

He nodded. "You know I'd do anything for you, pal."

Beth Cooper walked past the counter. This bitch was never going to leave me alone. Every week, some new story about me appeared in the paper, or some new spin on the same story that had been playing in the press for weeks. The Glouster Video Scandal. My story. Kind of.

She shot me a glare. Then a scowl. "Jesus, did you dump her or what?"

Dad jerked his head up. Shit. I hadn't told him I knew about him and Beth. But I'd known as soon as I saw the video everyone thought was me and Beth.

"What?" He feigned ignorance like a pro. Lied like a god.

"It's okay, Dad. I know about you and Beth." He shook his head as if he was about to deny it. "Seriously. It's all good." He already knew I'd figured out he'd uploaded the videos.

"Are you trying to blackmail me?"

I laughed. "Would it work? You don't have two twenties to rub together." His face went ashen, eyes black. "Relax. I'm kidding. It's too late for me, but you...you have the keys to the castle still." World at his feet. "If you can keep Beth quiet and figure out how to siphon some money, you'll be able to walk away. Get out of that toxic environment."

I'd never really seen a fight between them or heard an argument. Dad said they always waited until I went to bed or until I was out, but he'd reported some serious doozies.

He shrugged. "I don't know how I would go about it." But I didn't buy it. He was the CFO at the law office. He had access to all the money, even though the reports went to Mom and the board. If anyone could figure it out, it was him. I was only surprised he hadn't thought of it himself. His sigh was long and deep, pained. "I'll stick it out."

"What about her?" I nodded to Beth who was still shooting daggers at me. "You just screwing around?"

He swallowed hard and the resulting gulp reminded me of how I'd been with Reese. God, was that only a couple months ago?

"I think it could be something. She makes me feel young again." I glanced at Beth once then back again. Stared at her arm for a couple of long seconds. I would've bet any money I had that she was wearing a Rolex. Mom's maybe? Or had he managed to get enough money to buy his mistress jewelry while I was spending my days sweating my balls off behind a charbroiler and a flat grill?

"That's great. Hey, Dad, did you give Beth one of Mom's watches?"

His face went red, and he looked down. "No. I put one on my Amex. Told her it was for me." He shuffled his head from one side to the other. "She doesn't mind as much when I buy things for myself."

With my new lifestyle, the money he'd spent on that watch would see me through for six months. I tried not to be bitter. It was his money. I hadn't earned it. He did.

"Well, I hope you and Beth are very happy together." I wanted to be the kind of son, the kind of person who was happy for him. Who meant it when I said I wanted him to be happy, but the resentment was hard to swallow. "I have to get back to work, Dad." He nodded and smiled. "You take care, son. I'll bring you some more money as soon as I can."

I didn't want him taking unnecessary chances helping me. I was figuring out how to live on what I made here and at the library. "No, Dad, it's all right. I'll be fine."

He smiled and I hoped the light in his eyes was pride. "Love you, pal."

I nodded and turned to walk into the kitchen. I watched him climb into his Lexus and a few minutes later, Beth left.

It took a week before Dad came back and asked me to sit with him. "How you doing, pal?"

He looked tired. Haggard. But smiling. It was nice to see him happy. "I'm good. You look good."

Something about his smile was deeper than I'd seen before. If that meant he was enjoying life, I was glad for him. "Thanks. I've been working out. Taking walks with… taking walks." He pushed an envelope across the table. "I need your help with something."

He explained the plan. To take some money off the top of each of the accounts on the pages inside the envelope. To send it to two off-shore accounts, both already set up in my name so Mom wouldn't suspect, and he would have deniability in case it went south, although I didn't realize the reason then. "It'll ruin your mother and we can be on a beach in Belize before she ever realizes how bad it is." He laughed. "And since you have to make the transfer to me in person, you'll get some stamps in your passport."

I had plenty, but I could see the hundred-dollar bills sticking out behind the flap of the envelope. And it was a thick envelope, too.

Oh fuck. The temptation was real.

"I can't, Dad." I should've run straight to my mother and told her. It was the right thing to do, just like standing beside me was the right thing for her to do. Another block piled onto my pile of temptation.

"Sure, you can, pal. It's us against her. It always has been. I just want to make sure we get what's ours, right?"

Oh, fuck. When he put it like that… but no. I couldn't. I wasn't a thief. This was my new self telling my former self to get back in the box and stay there. I pushed the envelope to his side of the table. "I can't do it, Dad."

He nodded and slid the envelope inside the pocket of his blazer. "That's disappointing." I hated that word. His fingers tapped against the table. "I don't understand your loyalty to her." After a few moments of staring at me, he stood. "If you change your mind." He dropped a hundred-dollar bill on the table. "There'll be plenty more where that came from."

And he walked out. It was a long time before I saw him again.

17

Reese

A rollercoaster week turned into a rollercoaster month. The house deal fell through. Which seemed like a sign. I walked into the bank, asked for a loan, and got one. Bought a house.

Then, because my life wasn't complicated enough, I quit my job. By email. Then got another one. Same day.

Now, I was sitting in an office filling out paperwork for the new firm of Kennedy & Son, Attorneys at Law, as an investigator. A job that paid more than I'd ever been paid in my life.

Ever.

The offices were posh, too. Opulent. Extravagant. Even mine. Which was on the floor below the one the lawyers worked on but was bigger than the apartment I shared with Beth in college. It had its own bathroom complete with a shower, an exercise bike, the obvious desk, chair, visitors' chairs, and sofa, along with a kitch-enette with my own single cup/full pot coffee maker combo.

I hadn't run into Ryder's mom yet—kind of hoped I wouldn't—but I expected she had more important things to do than welcome me to the payroll.

"Miss Winthrop?" I lifted my head from the very enthralling tax form I was filling out. A young woman with a sleek, severe hairstyle and sensible shoes stood in the doorway. "Mr. Kennedy was wondering if you could meet him downstairs in the lobby."

I nodded. Moment of truth. I hadn't seen him...not even sent or received a text since he'd left the house that day I'd called our relationship *catching up.*

The elevator ride was impossibly long, but it gave me time to get my head together. To wrap my mind around working with him every day and not touching him. To tamp down all my unrequited lust and repeat the mantra that I couldn't—wouldn't—sleep with the boss.

When the doors whooshed open, I was mantra shmantra. Only thing I wanted to do was throw myself against him, feel his body under my hands. Touch him like I owned him.

Pull it together, fool. This job was my saving grace. My escape from loneliness. A gateway to bonding with my friends and establishing relationships that would last. Even if one of them couldn't be with Ryder.

Who would've thought that kidnapping him would have led to all of this? I'd traded my fishnet stockings in for more traditional pantyhose and my tutu in for a pencil skirt. I'd even twisted my hair into a bun and strapped on a pair of black pumps I borrowed from Avery.

Ryder looked me up and down, cocked his head, and nodded. "This is new." I nodded because I couldn't speak. I'd never seen him in a suit before—a form-fitting, three-piece suit, with a silk tie and a starched shirt with pants that hugged and accentuated and...fuck! How the holy hell was I supposed to resist all that?

"I can be Harley Quinn after six." Although I had to say, I'd never been so uncomfortable in clothes. How Avery managed to dress like this every single day for class gave me a new admiration for my already quite admirable friend.

He grinned. "And here I thought you were going for Goth Witch Glenda from Oz." His gaze burned up and down my body. "This is good, too, though."

When he held out his hand, there was nothing I could do but take it. It didn't mean I was holding my boss's hand. It meant, my boss was carefully guiding me to whatever it was he wanted to show me. It was a safety measure really. A precaution to ensure his employee wasn't injured in the workplace. OSHA would be so proud.

We walked out of the building together, side by side, hands still joined. We could've been anyone other than who we were—two people on the edge of losing each other. Again. Spinning out of relationship control with only ourselves to stop the forward thrust. And I was screwed. Waxing poetic was more Felicity's style than mine.

On the sidewalk out front of the coffee shop at the

lower level of the building, he pulled out a chair for me then sat across the table and scraped his nail back and forth in a one-inch space across the wooden top. Not looking at me. Not touching me anymore. We sat quietly for about three minutes before he looked up. "I'm not broke anymore."

I nodded. "I see that."

"I don't want to go back to being the way I was before I was broke." He took a quick glance at me then shuttered his gaze back to the table.

"And how were you?" Just because one of us needed to fill the silence.

"Stupid. I made some mistakes." He blew out a short breath. "Hurt some people." I couldn't have moved if I wanted to. More than moving, I wanted to hear where he took this. I sat back in my chair and waited. He continued scraping the edge of the table. "There was a girl."

"All the best stories have a girl in them."

He nodded. "Not like this one."

My heart had its own new rhythm. Fast. Hard. If I had to choose a description, I would have called it desperate. Like me and every cell in my body. "And how was this one different?"

He shook his head. "She was perfect without acting like she was perfect." Oh, God. If this was just a line…it was working. "Beautiful without knowing it. So fucking sexy I couldn't breathe most of the time." He looked up. "Still can't." Now he sighed and a little corner of my gut churned. "And I lost her."

There were a hundred things I wanted to say, but I

couldn't put a single set of thoughts together to make a sentence. Instead, I sat. Quiet. Hands folded in my lap. Prim. Waiting.

"I didn't mean to hurt her. And now, I don't know…I mean, I think I've lost her for good this time." He shook his head and looked up at me.

"Well, you never know. Maybe you're looking at it all wrong." An ounce of weight lifted off my heart. "I heard she got a great new job that's going to keep her close." So much for not sleeping with him. If he glanced at me one more time with those big sad eyes, I might have thrown him on top of the table and had my wicked way with him right there on Dunne Avenue. "And she bought a house over on Hampstead. The family home, I heard." He didn't smile yet. "Pretty great memories in that house. The more recent ones especially."

"Yeah?" Almost a grin.

"Mm-hmm. So, what I'm saying is that"—I cleared my throat because even though I was rethinking all my mottos and mantras from the last decade and beyond, I was nervous as hell—"I think if you want her, now would be a good time to take your shot, you know? Aim for the fences. Try to put it between the uprights." I made the touchdown signal then pulled my arms back to my side and refolded my hands in front of me.

He stood and walked around the table to pull me to my feet. "Did you know that I find sports analogies very arousing?" There was nothing in the world I liked more than looking at his smile, except for maybe his eyes when he smiled. They sparkled. And if I would've died right then, it would have been as a very happy woman watching a man smile at her. I couldn't think of a better way to go.

Unless it was to keep him smiling at me. "We could, uh, run a two-minute drill?"

He rolled his eyes. "Weak."

"Come on. You can shoot for a hole in one." He shook his head. "Come from behind?" He was right. These were horrible, but yes. I knew when I talked sports, it flipped his horny switch. So, I might've looked some stuff up. "Fourth and goal. Make a play, Ryder."

He shook his head and pulled me close. "There is nothing about you I don't like right now." He ran his hand over my spine to my waist and flipped the tab on my exposed zipper. "Except this skirt. I think we could…find something a little less…constrictive. Don't want you passing out during the main event."

I grinned. "Oh, main event." I snapped my fingers. "Damn the missed opportunity."

He lowered his head and brought his lips to within a breath of mine. "I want to make the most of every opportunity with you, Reese. I want to be the man you deserve, the one you can't wait to get home to at night and the one you…" He kissed me now. Slow. Sensual. Deep. So deep warmth spread through my stomach, fanned out in waves. When he pulled back, he leaned his forehead against mine. "The one you want to kiss in the morning."

I had news for him. He already was that guy. He was so much more. And I wasn't too scared to tell him. He just didn't give me the chance. Instead, our mouths crashed together again and we were kissing like teenagers, a tangle of arms and hands, breaths mingling, moans in symphony.

Finally, I pulled away, shy, almost. "We should take this somewhere more private."

He nodded and smiled, then wiggled his eyebrows. "I have an office."

Probably one twice as big as mine, and I was sure, at some point, we'd christen both, but I didn't want it to be today. "I have an entire house."

And I liked the way that sounded.

He kissed me again. Quicker this time then checked his watch. "And we have a meeting with my mother in…ten minutes."

What? Meeting with his mother? News like that was designed to kill lust. To stop it dead. "Ten minutes?"

He nodded. "Yeah." This time, he led me into the building and as we stood at the elevator, he filled me in on what happened between his mom and dad. How he'd helped his mother outsmart his dad and save the family fortune because his father had made one mistake after another. Then come to say goodbye to Ryder, as if he just couldn't resist rubbing it in his face when he, the father, ran off with a woman the same age as the son.

"If he hadn't asked me to help him cheat Mom before, we would've lost everything. But he forgot to adjust the plan and change the name from mine to his." Vindication. Redemption. A total happiness I'd not seen in him before. Ever. Not even ten years ago.

18

Reese

$\mathcal{N}$othing in the world felt more right than being with Ryder. Even lunch with his mom wasn't a problem, although it did feel similar to what I assumed being led to the gallows would feel like. I smiled anyway. Pretended I wasn't scared shitless. Right up to the minute we stepped out of the elevator to find Mom waiting.

"Ms. Winthrop." She held out her hand. "Do you mind if I call you Reese?"

I shook my head because I had no words. Literally. Because she was smiling. Not threatening me with a prenup with venom in her voice. Now she reminded me of cotton candy. Ice cream. Sunshine.

"I wanted to thank you for the opportunity here." I waved my arm in a wide arc to indicate the entire office building, like some kind of Vanna White, Price is Right merchandise model.

She smiled. Smiled.

"And I wanted to apologize to you for our first meeting." She sighed. "As you can imagine, my marriage has long left a lot to be desired. I wasn't at my best the day we met." She shot a wink over my head at Ryder, who had his hand on my shoulder. "I would like for us to start over. To be friends."

"Of course." I nodded, managed a smile, and tried not to pass out from the heart palpitations induced by my stone cold shock.

Surreal. Crazy. Something right out of Walt Disney World with flying genies and magic carpet rides.

Ryder moved around me and kissed his mother's cheek. "Shall we?"

I nodded. Lunch with my boss/boyfriend and his mother/my other boss. A decade ago, we'd been in a very different place. Now we were chatting over a mixed green salad lightly drizzled with a vinaigrette dressing, crispy panini sandwiches with grilled chicken and avocado, and a fresh fruit sorbet that I could've died for. Not that the menu was important, but there wasn't a detail about this day I planned to forget. I etched every individual second into my memory. From the blue tie he wore to the red-soled pumps his mother slipped off under our table.

She was all elegance and smooth talk. And it was easy to see exactly from where Ryder got his people skills. Anytime the conversation lagged, she swung it around to me. Extracted details I didn't realize I was giving out. Like a dance. A well-choreographed dance, and Ryder and I followed her lead.

By the time we finished lunch and the plates were cleared away, we talked business for the rest of the afternoon. My first order of business was to hunt down her husband and his mistress, my former best friend. Someone had to answer for the money missing from the accounts and that someone had to be Mr. Kennedy. And it was time to clear Ryder's name.

I knew this was a test. For Ryder as much as for me. This was his mother's way of making sure Ryder wasn't just back for the money. And he knew it. Told me so as he drove me home.

"Maybe she's just protecting the business." It made sense to me. Unchecked, Ryder's dad would've ruined the business, Mrs. Kennedy, and her reputation. Now she was working with the cops—as much as a woman with her kind of power ever worked with the cops—to track down the man who'd tried to cheat all her clients while also working with the FTC to "determine" how this kind of thing managed to happen in their firm.

Ryder smiled and shook his head. "Just sit back and wait. Mom has magic. She's going to take every sin ever perpetrated in their marriage, and spin it, so it rests solely on his shoulders." He glanced at me from the side.

"You okay with all of that?" I didn't want to fail at my first assignment, but I also didn't want to do anything that would make this suck anymore for Ryder.

He didn't answer for a few seconds. "I don't know. Twice in my life, he was going to let me hang for what he did." He sighed. "But he's also the guy who taught me how to throw a football and how to make a paper airplane."

I hated to hear him so melancholy. "The ever underestimated art of folding paper to make flying machines."

It could have gone either way. He could've been angry I was making light of it when I'd been the one who asked the question, or he could've taken it the way I intended—a way to lighten the air in the car. He squeezed my hand. "Don't make fun. It's a whole skill set. Every fold is essential to the amount of flight time, airspeed, wind resistance. It's basic engineering and physics."

And somehow, he'd made that whole explanation sound like dirty talk and foreplay. "You make it sound so naughty." He shot me a side-eye and a grin then focused on the road again. It gave me a minute to think. To try to fix the things I'd done wrong. "When I said we were just catching up…"

"You don't have to, Reese."

"I know." We were back together. There was no reason to bring it all back up, but I needed him to know, needed him to understand some things about me, too. "When I said we were just catching up, I was scared. I didn't know if I could…get past what happened before."

He nodded.

"And I don't want you to think it's about the money you have or the job or…anything else. I'm in this car right now because of the man you are, not because of the car you drive." Oh, God. I needed him to believe me.

He didn't speak until he pulled into the driveway at my house. I'd had my furniture from California shipped, painted some walls, and made some changes since he'd been here last and I wanted to show him, but he seemed to only want to sit in the car.

"Reese." Hearing him say my name would never get old. Especially when he said it through a smile. It added something indescribable to the sound. "I dated a lot before I met you."

I could've done without the *a lot*, but I let him hold my hand between his. "I know."

He shook his head. "But at the same time, I feel like there's never been anyone else but you." His gaze held mine. His fingers touched me. His breath warmed me when he leaned in. "You've always been more than I deserved." And he kissed me. Brushed his lips over mine once then came back in again. "Always will be." And finally, he said the words I'd been dying to hear since we met. "I love you."

And now, all was right with the world.

19

Ryder

At some point, I was going to have to stop worshipping her. I figured the lust would stop on its own, but apparently, that was going to take longer than the six months we'd been back together. And it certainly wasn't going to happen while she was in a bikini on a beach in Jamaica, oiled and tanned, beautiful, but on alert.

She hadn't stopped staring at the yacht on the water, barely even noticed I was there. "Baby, you found him. He isn't going anywhere, and now we can relax."

The Jamaican Constabulary Force was on their way in boats out to pick up Dad and ship him back to the states to face the wrath of Mom, and the FBI. Both of whom were very interested in his activities immediately before he left the country.

The whole damned thing had taken too much time away from me and Reese. Between her chasing leads all across the southern part of North America, and the other cases she worked for the firm, we saw each other a few hours a week these days. This was our vacation. Our time together. Reese had done her job. Now it was all about us. Our future. And the little velvet ring box hidden between my shirts back in our room.

Once, not even that long ago, I never would've dreamed I could be so happy again. Certainly wouldn't have guessed I'd be proposing with a ring that didn't come from one of those machines outside the supermarket.

But here I was. And my heart was about to burst.

And I had friends again. By default, since Reese couldn't see much of her friends without them seeing me, but still, it had been a long time since I went to a game with the guys and it was nice. Especially since we were all a little more mature than before, but with Keaton and Finn and Jameson, there was always a minute of the day where we were ridiculous and child-like. Fortunately, Reese found it attractive.

She turned and lowered herself into the cabana chair, but kept a firm hand on the binoculars. She'd worked hard for this and didn't want to miss it. Couldn't blame her really.

But just when the first JCF boat pulled up to the yacht dad bought with my trust fund—money he hadn't put into the offshore accounts—she turned to me, wide-eyed, sunglasses on top of her head. She flipped them down. "I have to talk to you about something." The sentence came out as a single word. Then she chuckled and tried again. "I have to…we need to talk."

Oh, God. This look—like she was about to throw up—never meant anything good was about to happen. I sat up and faced her so our knees bumped. "Is everything okay?" If she was about to dump me, I needed to prepare for a parachute-free landing.

Instead of answering, reassuring me so that my heart didn't explode and my guts spill out the hole where my heart previously lived, she cleared her throat. "It's…this has been the best six months of my life."

Oh, God. She was dumping me. "Reese."

"I wasn't really close with my mom and my dad was gone before I could remember him. So, the concept of family for me is more…abstract." Now she wouldn't even look at me. The fear bubbling inside of me rumbled through my veins and I looked down at my arm, expecting a physical manifestation to have appeared. Was almost disappointed when it hadn't. I probably needed to come in out of the sun, but no way could I move right now. "But the other day when your mom took me to the club for lunch, she introduced me as the daughter she never had." A tear slipped down her cheek, and while I didn't really understand how that was a bad enough thing to make her cry, I reached to catch it with my thumb anyway.

She tilted her head so it rested in my hand, and I stroked her cheek with my thumb. I loved touching her skin. "I love you." Maybe if I said it enough—and I said it as often as I could—it would convince her to stay with me.

She nodded. "I know. I love you, too." She bit her lip and closed her eyes. But at least she'd said she loved me. No way could she dump me now.

Right?

I had to stop this now. "Reese, we are on one of the most beautiful beaches in the world, with a view of the arrest of the century." For me anyway. "And I just want to enjoy it with you. Let's save all the heavy stuff for tonight."

Finally, she nodded and I got a reprieve. For a couple hours anyway, but the hours flew past and it was night, talk-time, before I could figure out how to stop the tide from rolling in, the wind from blowing, and time from passing.

She stood in our room, her dress—white with gauzy material that went from shoulder to ankle—billowing in the breeze from the open window she stood in front of. She didn't turn when I came out of the bathroom, didn't move when I got down on one knee beside her, and didn't smile when she finally turned to see me. But I was unde-terred. Nothing if not dogged in my determination.

Even when she swallowed hard and whispered an, "Oh, shit."

"Reese." My heart couldn't take much more of this. "Last year, I didn't think I was ever going to be happy again. I dreamed about holding you again, looking into your eyes, kissing those lips." I was getting off track. But I meant everything I said. "When I'm with you, I'm the man I want to be. And you make me better than I am." Moment of truth... "I love you so much, will you marry me?" I popped open the ring box and held it out.

And then I waited. Because she didn't answer. Hell, I wasn't even sure she was breathing. Still, I held my arm in the air like an idiot. Like a fucking fool about to get his heart broken because she didn't feel the same way, although she always acted like she did.

Granted things the last couple weeks had been strained. She was working hard. Tired because of it. But I never dreamed she wouldn't feel the same way, that this wasn't the way she expected our relationship to head.

Maybe she didn't expect it so soon. Maybe six months wasn't long enough. Maybe—

"I'm pregnant, Ryder." She closed her eyes and took a step backward.

"With a baby?" Not my brightest shining hour.

But she refrained from commentary more than a nod.

"How far?" Not that it mattered. Not to me. Probably it mattered. To a doctor, definitely. "Is everything okay? Have you been to the doctor? How do you know?" I found my voice and apparently, I had questions.

"A month or so. And I feel okay so far, a little nauseated in the morning. I made an appointment with the doctor for next week. And…" She reached into the pocket of her dress and pulled out four little sticks. Each one had a plus sign in the little window. "I didn't plan this."

I finally stood because still kneeling with my arm out in front of me and the ring box flipped open made me feel pathetic since she hadn't answered and wasn't likely to now.

"I know that." Of course, she hadn't planned it. She was the condom gatekeeper. I couldn't count the number of times she'd repeated her *no glove, no love* rule. "Condoms are only ninety-nine percent effective. Welcome to the one percent, sweetheart." The news hadn't really sunk in yet, but I could feel a smile building. A baby. Half me. Half her. All ours.

"Who said they're only ninety-nine percent?" Her brow furrowed and her eyes narrowed.

"The box, the manufacturer, tenth-grade health class, and every PSA and soap opera with a premarital sex story-line." Certainly, this couldn't be a newsflash for her. And then it occurred to me… "You don't want a baby?"

She laid her hand over her stomach, protective, motherly. "I do, I just thought we should have time first to be a couple." She looked down. "We're having a baby." Then she smiled and pulled her lower lip between her teeth. "We're going to be parents."

Parents. Us. Me. "Yeah. Wow, right?"

She blinked a couple times then smiled. "Married and a baby. So fast." She wrinkled her nose. "But so perfect."

She flipped faster than a fish on the deck. "Do you want to get married? Because you…never really answered." I would know because the waiting almost killed me. I was just now starting to breathe normally again from that first shock. The second one still hadn't hit yet. Or maybe it wouldn't because making a family with her was the right thing. The perfect thing.

"Of course, I want to get married. I just didn't think you were ever going to get around to asking. That's why I was going to do it on the beach today."

Relief swirled through me. Holy fuck. It made smiling, pulling her close, kissing her softly before I spoke easier. "That's what that was?"

"Yeah." She rested her hands on my shoulders and looked up at me as I pulled her closer. "I love you, Ryder."

"I love you." And I loved our future and our family, and for as long as I lived, there would never be another woman for me but this one. My one true love.

DARK DESIRES
~ A billionaire dark romance series ~
Dark Desire
Dark Rules
Dark Secret
Dark Time
Dark Truth

BARRE TO BAR
~ A billionaire second chance series ~
Dancing With Lies
Dancing With Temptation
Dancing With Doubt
Dancing With Guilt
Dancing With Redemption

TWISTED INTENTION

~ A billionaire revenge romance series ~
Twisted Beauty
Twisted Love
Twisted Fate

Mafia's Obsession
~ A hot mafia romance series ~
Mafia's Dirty Secret
Mafia's Fake Bride
Mafia's Final Play

Screaming Demons
~ An MC romance series full of suspense ~
Rough Start
Rough Ride
Rough Choice
Rough Patch
Rough Return
Rough Road
Rough Trip
Rough Night
Rough Love

Standalone Contemporary Romance
Billionaire in Vegas
Billionaire Hunt
Billionaire's Game
Billionaire Retreat
Billionaire On Air

A Chance To Love
Somebody To Love
Not Mine To Love

Check out Summer's entire collection at
www.summercooper.com/books

ABOUT SUMMER COOPER

Thank you so much for reading. Without you, it wouldn't be possible for me to be a full-time author. I hope you enjoy reading my books as much as I do writing them.

Besides (obviously!) reading and writing, I also love cuddling my dogs, shouting at Alexa, being upside down (aka Yoga) and driving my family cray-cray!

Get in touch at
hello@summercooper.com
www.summercooper.com

facebook.com/summercooperauthor
instagram.com/summercooperauthor
goodreads.com/summercooper
bookbub.com/profile/summer-cooper